The Soul Thieves

Catherine Fisher

The Soul Thieves

THE BODLEY HEAD
London

1 3 5 7 9 10 8 6 4 2

Copyright © Catherine Fisher 1996

Catherine Fisher has asserted her right under the Copyright,
Designs and Patents Act, 1988 to be identified as the author of
this work.

First published in the United Kingdom 1996
by The Bodley Head Children's Books
Random House, 20 Vauxhall Bridge Road, London SW1V 2SA

Random House Australia (Pty) Limited
20 Alfred Street, Milsons Point, Sydney,
New South Wales 2061, Australia

Random House New Zealand Limited
18 Poland Road, Glenfield,
Auckland 10, New Zealand

Random House South Africa (Pty) Limited
PO Box 337, Bergvlei 2012, South Africa

Random House UK Limited Reg. No. 954009

A CIP record for this book is available from the British Library

ISBN 0 370 31249 0

Phototypeset by Intype, London
Printed in Great Britain
by Mackays of Chatham, PLC

For Tess

All chapter-head quotations are taken from
Voluspa, translated as *The Song of the Sybil*
in Norse Poems, edited and translated by
W H Auden and Paul Taylor.
Faber and Faber Ltd.

1

*Outside I sat by myself
when you came.*

The sword was of heavy beaten iron, with a narrow
groove down the centre of the blade. On the
pommel, tiny gilt birds with red eyes watched each
other, and two dragons wound their bodies round
the hilt, notched and scratched.

'It's not new,' Brochael observed.

'It's perfect.' Hakon's voice was so stunned that
almost no-one heard him. He looked up at the house-
thrall who had brought it. 'Tell Wulfgar . . . tell the
Jarl that I'm grateful. Very grateful.'

The man went and whispered his message in the
Jarl's ear, and they saw Wulfgar grin and wave lazily
down the long crowded table.

Hakon held the sword tight, turned it over,
scratched with his thumb-nail at a tiny mark in the
metal. His right hand, still slightly smaller and
weaker than the left, clasped the hilt; he slashed with
it sideways, at imaginary enemies.

Jessa jerked back, 'Be careful!'

'Sorry.' Reluctantly, he laid the sword on the table,
among the greasy dishes. Jessa smiled to herself. She
knew he barely believed it was his.

'Better than that rust-heap you had before,' Brochael said, emptying the last drop of wine thoughtfully onto the floor. 'Now it needs a name.' He reached over for the jug and re-filled his cup. 'And here's the very man. What are some good names for a sword, Skapti?'

The tall poet lounged on the end of the bench.

'Whose is it?'

'Hakon's.'

Skapti touched the blade with his long fingers. 'Well,' he said, considering, 'you could call it Growler, Angry One, Screamer, Rune-Scored, Scythe of Honour, Worm-Borer, Dragonsdeath . . .'

'I like that one.'

'Don't interrupt.' Skapti glared at him. 'Leg-Biter, Host-Striker, Life-Quencher, Corpse-Pain, Wound-Bright, Skull-Crusher, Deceiver, Night-Bringer . . . Oh, I could go on and on. There are hundreds of sword-names. The skald-lists are full of them.'

'You can't name it until it's done something,' Jessa said firmly. She poured Skapti some wine.

'You mean killed someone?' Hakon sounded uneasy.

'Drawn blood.' Brochael winked over the boy's head. 'The blade must drink, that's what they say. Then you name it.'

Skapti tapped the hilt. 'Where did you get it?'

A burst of laughter along the table rang in the noisy hall. Then Hakon said, 'Wulfgar gave it to me. To mark his wedding.' He reached out and touched it lightly, and the firelight glittered in the metal, like a splash of blood.

Jessa shivered then, though the mead-hall was warm and smoky, and her scarlet dress heavy and

2

spun of good wool. For a moment even the clatter of dishes and conversation seemed to fade; then the foreboding passed, and the talk rose about her again.

She looked along the table.

Wulfgar sat in the middle, leaning forward in his carved chair, his dark coat edged with fur at the collar. He was listening as Signi whispered something close to his ear; then he smiled and closed his hand over hers.

'Look at him,' Jessa laughed. 'Oblivious.'

'Ah well, I don't blame him,' Brochael said dryly. 'She's a fine girl.'

Fine was the word, Jessa thought. Signi's hair was long and fine, delicate as spun silk, pale and golden. Her dress moved as she turned on the seat; gold glinting at her wrist and shoulders. A fine girl, refined; the daughter of a wealthy house. They had been betrothed to each other for years; since they were both children, Jessa knew. And now Wulfgar had come into his land and power, now he was Jarl, they were to be married. Tomorrow at noon. Midsummer's Day.

The table was thronged with Signi's family and kin; they had been travelling in all week from outlying farms. Wulfgar's friends had made room for them; the Jarl's guests always had pride of place.

Jessa looked round at Brochael. 'Is Kari still asleep? Perhaps we should wake him.'

He frowned down at her, then looked across the room towards the door. 'If you like. There won't be anything left to eat if he doesn't come soon. But you know how he is, Jessa, he may not want to come.'

She nodded, standing. 'I'll go up and see.'

Crossing the hall, between the tables, she dodged

3

the serving men and thought that Kari could hardly be asleep. The noise of the Jarl's feast was loud, and all the doors were open to the light midsummer night, the sun barely setting even now, the pale sky lit with eerie streaks of cloud. At this time of year it never really got dark at all. She slipped through the archway, up the stone stairs, and along to a room at the end, where she tapped on the door.

'Kari?'

After a moment he answered her. 'Come in, Jessa.'

He was sitting in front of the dying fire, his back against the bench and his knees drawn up. Firelight lit his pale face with red, leaping glimmers; his hands were red, and his hair, and for a moment she thought again that it looked like blood, and went cold.

He glanced up, quickly. 'What is it? What's the matter?'

'Nothing.' She came inside. 'It was just the light on you. It's dark in here.'

He looked back at the fire. 'You were scared for a minute. I felt it.'

The two black ravens that followed him everywhere stood on the windowsill, looking out. One of them stared strangely at her.

She perched on the bench, rubbing her foot. 'I'm never scared. Now are you coming down? Brochael's eating and drinking for ten, but there's still plenty left.'

'Has Wulfgar asked for me?'

'No. He knows you.' If it had been anyone else, she knew, Wulfgar would have taken their absence as a deliberate insult, but not Kari. Kari was different.

His mother was the witch, Gudrun, the Snow-walker. After he was born she had locked him away

4

for six years, never allowing him to be seen, but he had grown to be as powerful as she was, and to look like her, so that the people of the hold made him uneasy, with their covert, frightened glances. Kari avoided crowds, and Jessa understood why.

Now he made no attempt to move, his best blue shirt picking up soot-smuts from the dirty floor.

'There's nothing wrong, is there?' she asked, anxiously.

He pushed the long silvery hair back from his eyes. 'No.' But he sounded puzzled, not quite sure.

'Tell me,' she said after a moment.

Turning to her, his face was drawn, uneasy. 'Oh, I don't know, Jessa. It's just that tonight, since the twilight began, I've felt something. A tingling in my fingers. A shiver. Coldness. It worries me that I can't think what it is.'

'Do you think it's this wedding?'

'No. I think it's just me.' Suddenly he stood, pulling her up. 'I'm hungry. Let's go down. I'd like to see Hakon's new sword.'

Jessa stopped dead. 'He's only just been given it. How did you . . .'

His pleading look silenced her.

As they walked up the crowded hall a ripple of hush followed them, as if conversations had faltered and then gone rapidly on. People were only just beginning to get used to Kari; it took them such a long time, Jessa thought irritably. His pale skin and frost-grey, colourless eyes disturbed them; when they saw him they remembered Gudrun, and were afraid.

But Wulfgar was pleased. 'So you came!' he said, lazily. 'I wondered if we'd have the honour.'

5

Kari smiled back, glancing at Signi. 'I'm sorry. Brochael says I have no manners; he's right.'

The blonde girl looked at him curiously. Then she poured him a cup of wine and held it out. 'I'm glad you've come, Kari,' she said, in her soft, southland accent. 'You and I need to be friends. I want to know all Wulfgar's friends. I want them to like me.'

He took the cup, his eyes watching her face. 'They will, lady.'

She flushed, glancing at Wulfgar. 'Is that a prophecy?'

Wulfgar laughed, and Kari said, 'It's already come true.'

He raised the cup to drink and stopped; so still that Jessa looked at him. He was staring into the wine as if something had poisoned it, and when he looked up his face was white with terror.

'She's here,' he breathed.

Alarmed, Wulgar leaned forward. 'Who is?'

But Kari had spun round, quick as a sword-slash. 'Close the doors!' he yelled, his voice raw and desperate over the hubbub. 'Close them! NOW!'

Skapti was on his feet; Wulfgar too.

'Do it!' he thundered, and men around the hall moved, scrambling from tables, grabbing their weapons. Jessa caught Kari's arm and the red wine splashed her dress.

'What is it?' she gasped. 'What's happening?'

'She's here.' He stared over her shoulder. 'Gods, Jessa. Look!'

Mist was streaming through the high windows; strange glinting stuff, full of shadows and forms, hands that came groping over the sills, figures that

6

swarmed in the doorways. In seconds the hall was full of it, an icy silver breath that swirled and blinded.

Women screamed; angry yells and barking and sword-play rang in the crowded, panic-stricken spaces. The fires shrivelled instantly, hard and cold; candles on the table froze. The mist swirled between faces, and people were lost; Jessa saw Wulfgar tugging at his sword, then he was gone, blanked out by a wraith of fog that caught her and seemed to drag her by the arms. She tore herself away and somewhere nearby Kari called out; then he was shoved against her so hard they both fell, crashing against the table. She grabbed him and screamed 'Kari!', but he didn't answer, and putting her hand to his face her fingers felt wetness. She held them near to her eyes and saw blood.

'Kari!'

In the uproar no-one heard her. Pale unearthly forms of men and dogs moved around her; a sword slapped down hard nearby as men fought amongst themselves, against their shadows. She scrambled up and was knocked back by a blow from something cold and hard; crumpling on hands and knees she felt the side of her face go numb and tingle; then the pain grew to a throbbing ache.

Someone grabbed her; she flung him off but he gasped, 'It's me!'

She recognized the sword. 'Hakon! What's happening?'

'I don't know.'

'Kari's hurt. We need to get him somewhere safe!'

They felt for him in the mist and grabbed him under the arms; then Hakon dragged him back under

7

the table, kicking benches out of the way. They crouched over him, shocked.

'It's Gudrun!' Jessa stormed.

'What?'

'Gudrun! She's doing this!'

Around them the mist closed in. Shapes moved in it; they thought they saw huge men, tall as trolls, creatures from nightmares. A fog-wolf with glinting eyes snarled under the table; the legs of distorted, monstrous beings waded past them through the hall. Frost was spreading quickly across the floor; it crunched under their feet and nails; they breathed it in and the pain of it seared their throats, clogged their voices.

'Getting cold,' Hakon's voice whispered, close to her.

'Me too.' She struggled to say 'Keep awake' but her lips felt swollen, her tongue would not make the sounds.

Cold stiffened her clenched fingers.

'Hakon . . .' she murmured, but he did not answer. She felt for him; his arm lay cold beside her.

Around them the hall was silent.

Now the white grip of the ice was creeping gently over her cheek, spreading on her skin. With a great effort she shifted a little, and the fine film cracked, but it formed again almost instantly, sealing her lips with a mask of glass. She couldn't breathe.

Crystals of ice closed over her eyelids, crusting her lashes.

Darkness froze in her mind.

2

A farseeing witch, wise in talismans,
Caster of spells.

Lost in the frost-spell, each of them walked in a dream. Brochael dreamt he was in some sort of room. He was sure of that, but couldn't remember how he had come there. He was holding open a heavy door; a chain swung from it, rusted with age. In his other hand was a lantern; he raised it now, to see what was there.

In the darkness, something made a sound. He swung the light towards it.

It was squatting on the floor, pressed into a corner. A small, crouched shape, twisting away from the light. Heavily, Brochael crossed the dirty straw towards it. The door closed behind him.

The red flame of the lantern quivered; he saw eyes, a scuttle of movement.

It was a boy, about six years old. He was filthy, his hair matted and soiled, his clothes rags. Crusts of dirt smeared his thin face; his eyes were large, staring, without emotion.

Brochael crouched, his huge shadow enveloping the corner of the stinking cell. The boy did not move.

'Can you speak?' He found his voice gruff; anger

mounting in him like a flame. When the boy made no answer he reached out for him. With that trembling touch he knew this was Kari; he remembered, and looked up, and saw Gudrun there. She put out her hand and pulled the boy up; he changed, grew older, cleaner, taller, so that they faced each other, among the shadows.

The lantern shook in Brochael's hand.

He could not tell them apart.

Hakon dreamed himself in a white emptiness. As he reached for his sword it slid away from him; alarmed, he grabbed it and the whole floor rose up beneath him, became a surface of glass, slippery, impossible to grip. Desperately, palms flat, he slipped down, down into Gudrun's spell, and below him was an endless roaring chasm, deep as his nightmares.

An idea came to him, and he stabbed the sword into the ice to hold himself steady, but out of it wriggled a snake that wound around his hand, the cool scales rippling between his fingers. He lost power and feeling; the fingers were forced wide and the snake gripped his wrist so tight the sword fell from his numb fingers; it toppled over the brink, and fell, and he fell after it, into nowhere.

Skapti's nightmare was very different. For him it meant standing in a green wood, watching the mist from a distance. He knew it was a spell. Shapes moved in it; his friends, he thought, each of them lost.

Under his long hand the bark of the tree was rough; leaves were pattering down around him in the wind – at least he thought at first they were

10

leaves, but as he looked at them again he saw they were words. All the words of all his songs were coming undone and falling about him like rain. He caught one and crunched it in his fingers; a small, crisp word.

Lost.

He let it fall, angrily, chilled to the heart.

Then he saw her standing in the wood; a tall white-skinned woman laughing at him. 'Poets know a great deal, Skapti,' she said, 'and make fine things. But even these can be destroyed.'

As he stared at her the words fell between them, a silent, bitter snow.

Signi had no idea she was dreaming. A tall woman bent over her and helped her stand.

'Thank you,' she murmured, brushing her dress. 'What happened? Where's Wulfgar?'

The woman smiled, coldly, and before Signi could move she fixed a narrow chain of fine cold links to each of her wrists. Signi stared at her, then snatched her hands away. 'What are you doing?'

She gazed round in horror at the frozen hall. 'Wulfgar!'

'He won't hear you.' The woman turned calmly, leading her out; Signi was forced to follow. She tugged and pulled, but it was no use. 'Where are we going?' she asked, fearfully.

Gudrun laughed.

As they left the hall it rippled into nothing, into mist.

Wulfgar knew he had lost her. In his dream he ran through the empty hold looking for her, calling her

11

name. Where was everyone? What had happened? Furious, he stopped and yelled for his men.

But the night was silent; the aurora flickering over the stone hall and its dragon-gables. He raced down to the fjord-shore, and ran out onto the longest wharf, his boots loud on the wooden boards.

'Signi!' he yelled.

The water was pale, lit by the midnight sun. Only as he turned away did he see her, fast asleep under the surface. Eels slithered through her hair, the fine strands spreading in the rise and fall of the current. When he lay down and reached out to her, thin layers of ice closed tight about his wrist.

The water held him, a cold grip.

Only Kari did not dream. Instead he slipped out of his body and stood up, looking down at the blood on his hair. Then he edged between the fallen tables and the dream-wrapped bodies of his friends to the door of the hall, flung wide. Outside the watchman lay sprawled, his sword iced over, the black wolfhound stiff at his side.

Stepping over them, Kari hurried out under the dawn-glimmer and looked north. Down the tracks of the sky he watched shapes move; heard voices call to him from invisible realms. He answered, quickly, and the ghosts of jarls and warriors and women came and crowded about him.

'What happened?' he asked, bitterly.

'She came. She took one of them back with her.'

'Who came?'

They stared at him, their faces pale as his. 'We know no names. Names are for the living.'

'You must tell me!'

12

'She. The Snow-walker.'

His mother. He wondered why he'd been so urgent; he'd known it would be her. He nodded and turned back slowly, and they made room for him, drifting apart like mist.

Coming back into the hall he gazed across it, at the frosted trunk of the roof-tree, where it stood rising high into the rafters. Two black forms sat among its branches.

'Go out and look,' he said. 'There may be some trace of her. Look to the North.'

'It's unlikely,' one of them croaked.

'Try anyway. I'll wake these.'

As they rose up and flapped out of the window he moved, reluctantly, back into his body, feeling the heavy pain begin to throb in his head, the bitter cold in fingers and stomach.

He rolled over, dragging himself up unsteadily onto his knees, fighting down sickness. Then he grabbed Jessa's arm and shook it, feebly. 'Jessa! Wake up. Wake up!'

It was all a dream, Jessa knew that. She stood on the hilltop next to the grazing horse and looked down at the snow-covered land. Fires burned, far to the south. A great bridge, like a pale rainbow, rose up into the sky, its end lost among clouds.

On the black waters of the fjord she was watching a ship, a funeral ship, drift on the ebb tide. Even from here she could see the bright shields hung on each side of it, and they were burning, their metal cracking and melting, dropping with a hiss into the black water. Flames devoured the mast, racing up the edges of the sails.

13

And on the ship were all the friends she knew and had ever known, and they were alive. Some were calling out to her, others silent, looking back; Skapti and Signi, Wulfgar and Brochael, Marrika and Thorkil, her father, Kari, Hakon with his bright new sword, and looking so desolate that her heart nearly broke.

Gudrun was standing beside her. The witch was tall; her long silver hair hung straight down her back.

'My ship,' she said softly. 'And if you want them as they were, Jessa, you must come and get them.'

'Come where?' Jessa asked, furious.

'Beyond the end of the world.'

'There's nothing beyond the end!'

'Ah, but there is.' Gudrun smiled her close, secret smile. 'The land of the soul. The place beyond legends. The country of the wise.'

Then she reached out and gripped Jessa's arm, painfully.

'But now you must wake up.'

And it wasn't Gudrun, it was Kari, his face white, blood clotted in his hair. He leaned against her and she struggled up from the floor, holding his arm. Ice cracked and splintered and fell from her hair and clothes; she felt cold, cold to the heart.

'What happened? You look terrible!'

'I hit my head,' he said quietly. 'I can't see properly.'

Making him sit down she stared around. The hall was dim, lit only with the weak night sun and a strange frosty glimmer. A film of ice lay over everything; over the floor, the tables, the sprawled bodies of the sleepers, over plates of food and upturned benches. Wine was frozen as it spilt; the fires were out, hard and black, and on the walls the tapestries were stiff, rigid folds.

In the open doorway she could see where the mist had poured in and turned to ice; it had frozen in rivulets and glassy, bubbled streams, hard over tables and sleeping dogs. The high windows were sheeted with icicles.

No wonder no-one had been ready. Swords were frozen into scabbards; shields to their brackets on the walls. A woman lay nearby holding a child, both of them white with frost and barely breathing.

Jessa shivered. 'We've got to wake them! They'll die otherwise.'

He nodded, stood up and walked unsteadily to the fires. As she shook Hakon fiercely she heard the crackle and stir of the rune-flames igniting behind her.

It took a long time to wake everyone. Some were deep in the death-sleep, almost lost in their dreams, their souls wandering far among spells. Brochael awoke with a jerk, gripping her shoulder; Skapti more slowly, raising his head from the table and looking upwards, as if the roof was falling in.

Gradually the hall thawed and filled with noise; murmurs grew to voices, angry, questioning; small children sobbed and the warmth from the fires set everything dripping and softening.

'Get those doors shut!' Brochael ordered. One arm around Kari, he parted the boy's hair. 'That's deep. Get me something, Hakon, to stop the blood.'

'Where's Wulfgar?' Jessa ran to the high table. It was overturned on its side. A knife had been flung in the confusion and was frozen, embedded in the wood. She scrambled over, tugging benches and chairs away, crunching the frozen straw underneath. She saw his arm first, flung round Signi, and with a yell to Skapti she tried to drag the heavy table off them, until men came and pushed her aside, heaving the boards away, crowding round the Jarl.

They helped him sit up, breathless and sore.

'What was it?' he managed.

Jessa crouched. 'It looks like Gudrun's work. Some sort of spell. A few people are hurt, but none are dead. Are you all right?'

He rubbed soot and ice from his face and nodded, turning to Signi. She lay cold on the straw, Skapti bending over her. The skald looked up, anxiously. 'I can't wake her.'

Wulfgar grabbed the girl's shoulders, his hands crushing the fine silk. 'Signi!' He shook her again.

She lay still, still as death, but they saw she was breathing. Her face was clear, and her eyes opened, but there was no movement in her, no flicker of recognition.

'Signi?' Wulfgar said again. 'Are you all right?'

When she still did not speak he lifted her, and Jessa righted a chair and they sat her in it, but her head lolled slowly to one side, the long hair swinging over her face.

A woman began to cry, in the crowd.

Wulfgar chafed her hands. 'Get her waiting-women. Get Einar . . .'

'It's no use.'

Kari's voice was harsh, and they turned, surprised. He stood by the table, Brochael's great arm around him.

'What do you mean?' Wulfgar yelled.

16

'She's gone. Gudrun has taken her.'

'Taken her!' The Jarl leapt up. 'She's not dead!'

'Not even that. Taken her soul, taken it far away.' He put his hand to his head as if it ached, and for a moment Jessa thought he would fall, but he looked up again and nodded at the centre of the hall. 'Look. She left her mark.'

The roof-tree was split, from top to bottom.

Carved deep in the wood a white snake twisted, poison bubbling and hissing from its jaws.

3

The gods hastened to their hall of judgement,
Sat in council to discover who
Had tainted all the air with corruption...

They carried Signi upstairs and laid her on the bro-
caded bed in her room, with a warm fur cover over
her and the fire crackling over the new logs. But
nothing they did could wake her, no voice, no
entreaty. She breathed shallowly, so slowly that it
frightened them, and both the herb-woman, Gerda,
and the physician, Einar Grimsson, tried every
remedy they knew, filling the chamber with exotic
scents of oils and unguents and charred wood. They
even tried pricking her skin with sharp needles, but
she never moved, though the red blood ran freely.
Finally Wulfgar stopped it all and ordered them out.

When Jessa tapped on the door a little later, he
was still sitting on the edge of the bed, his wine-
stained coat held tight around him.

'Well?' he said, without turning.

She came into the room, Skapti behind her.

'Kari says it was some kind of supernatural attack.'
The skald leaned against the shuttered window. 'I
think he's right – there are no footprints outside, no
horse tracks, no evidence of any armed force.'

18

'But we saw them! Some of the men are wounded.'

'I know, but what we saw were visions, Wulfgar, mind-shapes, nothing that was real. Everyone seems to have seen different things. Some of the men may have fought each other, or against wraiths and shadows – none of us knew what was real. We were all spell-blinded.'

'Can you remember,' Jessa said slowly, 'what you dreamed?'

Skapti looked at her, absently. 'No. Not really. Except that it was full of pain.'

Wulfgar got up suddenly and stormed around the room. 'How could she do this! And why Signi? She's never even met Gudrun! If the witch wanted revenge on us why didn't she kill us all there in the hall?'

Jessa stirred, on the bench by the fire. 'This is what she said she would do.'

They both stared at her blankly, so she dragged the loose brown hair from her cheek and said, 'Don't you remember the night we all saw her, in that strange vision? The night the creature came? She was standing in a snow-field. She said she wanted Kari to come to her, and he wouldn't. Then she turned to you.'

'I remember.' Wulfgar stared darkly across the room. 'She said "What you love best, that thing I will have." But I never thought it would be this.'

He looked down at the girl on the bed. Her eyes were closed now, as if she slept.

'Sit down,' Skapti said gently. 'We need to think.'

Wulfgar came over and slumped beside Jessa on the bench. All his usual lazy elegance had left him. He put his head in his hands and stared hopelessly into the fire. 'What can we do?'

Neither of them could answer.

In the awkward silence they heard footsteps outside. Then Brochael opened the door and ushered Kari in.

The boy looked frail; he went and gazed down at Signi and they saw the deep raw cut across his forehead.

'You should be in bed,' Wulfgar muttered.

'That's what I said,' Brochael growled.

Ignoring them both, Kari came and sat by the blazing logs.

'What do we do?' Wulfgar said again.

Kari watched him bleakly. Then he said, 'It's only too clear what we have to do. Gudrun has made sure we have no choice. We have to go to her.'

'Why?'

'Because that's where Signi is.' He glanced again at the still shape on the bed. 'That isn't her, it's just her body, her shell. It's empty. She's not there.'

'How do you know?'

'Because I've been into her mind, Wulfgar, and it's blank!' He ran long fingers through his hair and then said, 'Gudrun has done this to make me come to her.'

'Come where?' Jessa asked, remembering her dream.

'I don't know. Far away.'

'The land of the White People.'

He shrugged. 'Wherever that is.'

Skapti came forward, intrigued. 'They say it's beyond the end of the world. A place of trolls, a giant-haunt. They say the ice goes up to touch the sky. No-one could live up there.'

20

'The snow-walkers live there. My people,' said Kari, grimly.

Wulfgar looked up suddenly. 'All right. If you say that's what we have to do to get her back, we'll do it. I'll take as many ship-loads of men as I can get; a war-band . . .'

'A war-band is no use,' Brochael said, unexpectedly. His huge shadow loomed on the wall, the firelight warm on his tawny hair and beard. 'The last Jarl sent a war-band up there and no-one ever came back.

'He's right,' Kari said. 'Besides, only I need to go.'

There was an uproar of protest, everyone speaking at once until Brochael's strong voice silenced them. 'You can't go! Even if you got there, she'd kill you!'

'She could have killed me here.' Calmly Kari rubbed his forehead. 'She doesn't want that. She wants me alive.'

'You're not going!' Brochael was angry now and obstinate; his face was set.

'There's no alternative.' Kari looked at him hard. 'Think of it, Brochael. Signi will just lie like that for months, for years, never speaking, never knowing any of us. We could all grow old and die, and she'd just be the same. Gudrun has plenty of time. Gudrun can wait for us.'

Silent with pain, Wulfgar clenched his fingers.

But stubbornly the big man shook his head. 'It's folly. She may wake; we don't know.' He came over and crouched down, his strong hands on the boy's shoulders. 'And I didn't bring you out of her prison for this. I don't want you to go.'

'I have to.' Kari's eyes were clear and cold; he looked like Gudrun, that secret, tense look.

Brochael stood up and stalked across the room to the door. He slammed his fist against the wood.

'We've never quarrelled before,' Kari said, bleakly.

'And we're not now. If you go over the world's edge I'm going with you, and you know that well enough. But we're walking into her trap. How could she steal the girl's soul!'

Kari was quiet for a moment. Then he said, 'She's learned how. She's been powerful for too long.'

Brochael's scowl deepened. He glared at the poet. 'You're very quiet. You usually have some opinion.'

The skald shrugged thin shoulders. 'I think Kari is right, we have no choice. And for a poet, such a journey is enticing. A dream-road. They say there are lands of fire and ice up there. Someone would have to make the song of it, and it might as well be me.'

'I won't be left behind either,' Jessa said firmly. 'Don't even think it. I'm coming.'

Her scowl made them all smile, even now. When Jessa made up her mind they all knew nothing would shift her.

Wulfgar stirred. 'Then it's settled. A small group of us — we'll travel more quickly and secretly that way, and need less . . .'

They glanced at each other, wondering who would say it. Finally Skapti did. 'Not you,' he said quietly.

Wulfgar stared at him.

'Skapti's right,' Jessa leaned forward. 'You can't come with us, Wulfgar. You know that. Your place is here.'

'My place,' he breathed, 'is with Signi.'

'It isn't. It can't be.' She stood up and faced him. 'Look, I'll tell you this straight out, as no-one else

22

will. You're the Jarl. You rule the land, keep the peace, settle the disputes. You order the trade, keep the frontiers, hunt down outlaws. The people chose you. You can't turn your back on them. If you came with us and we were away months, even years, what would be here when we came back?' She smiled at him, sadly. 'Famine, blood-feuds, cattle-raiding. Black, burned farms. A wasteland.'

He looked away from her; such a hard, desolate look as she had never seen on him before. The room was silent. Only the flames crackled over the logs. Then Wulfgar looked back at her bitterly. 'I think I'll never forgive you for this, Jessa.'

'You will.' She sat down and tried to smile at him. 'And think of it this way. When she wakes, it's you she'll want to see.'

4

When Ymir lived, long ago.

All the next day Wulfgar avoided everybody. He spent hours sitting in Signi's room, watching her still face, or staring silently out of the window. At mealtimes he was irritable. Finally, late in the afternoon, he called for his horse and galloped away from the hold, riding hard for the hills.

Jessa watched him go, leaning against the corner of the hall. She could guess how he felt; Wulfgar was impulsive, always the one to act. It would be very hard for him to stay behind.

Over her shoulder, Skapti said, 'The trouble with him is that he knows you were right.'

'I wish I hadn't said anything. I should have let him think it out for himself.'

The skald laughed. 'Always spilling your wisdom, little valkyrie.' He turned her gently. 'Now let's go and see Kari, because I think he wants us. One of those spirit-birds of his just came and croaked at me. The creature almost ordered me in.'

She walked along beside him, gravely. 'Things are different in the daylight, aren't they?'

'Lighter, you mean?'

She thumped his arm. 'You know what I mean. Last night, in all that confusion, everything seemed

24

so unreal. Signi, those dreams, the cold. The idea of a journey seemed . . . exciting.' She looked down at the longships moored at the wharf. A chill breeze moved them. 'Now it's more frightening. It will be so cold up there. And no-one has ever come back, and even if we get there . . .'

'There's Gudrun.'

'Yes.' She looked up at him. 'Do you think it's the right thing to do?'

'I don't,' he said abruptly. 'But I think it's the only thing we can do.'

'Skapti, you're mad.'

'I'm a poet,' he said, opening the door of the hall. 'Pretty much the same thing.' He grinned at her, lopsided. 'You're not usually so wary.'

'Dreams,' she said, absently. 'Those dreams. They hang around.'

Kari was out of bed and sitting at a table near the fire, carving a small piece of bone into a flat disc. He looked up at them.

'At last!'

'Feeling better?' Jessa tipped his head sideways and examined the cut critically. 'Brochael was worried about you. He said you'd lost a pint of blood and you were a thin, bloodless wraith and couldn't afford it.'

Kari shrugged. 'He's given me orders not to stir out. That's why I sent the birds.'

One of them flapped in at the window just then, hopping awkwardly down from the sill. It had a red, dripping object in its beak that might once have been a stoat. Delicately the bird picked it apart.

'Corpse-carver,' Skapti murmured, ominously.

They were watching it when Brochael came back.

25

Hakon was with him; they staggered in carrying a large wooden chest.

'Just here,' Brochael grunted, putting his end down easily. Hakon dropped his with relief.

'No sword?' Jessa said sweetly, behind him.

He crumpled, breathless. 'Not in the hall. Jarl's orders. I can live for an hour without it.'

'Not much longer, though.'

'Now,' Brochael wrenched the key round in the rusted lock. 'This should be what we want.'

He put both hands to the lid and heaved it open; it crashed back on the leather hinges and a great cloud of brown dust billowed upwards.

'What's all that?' Jessa murmured, looking down.

'Maps. So Guthlac says.'

He began to rummage around with his great hands, tugging out rolls of withered brown parchment and skins, worn to dust at the edges, some of them tied and sealed with red, crumbling wax.

'Clear that table,' he muttered. 'Let's see what's in here.'

Each of them dipped in and took a handful of skins, unfolding them carefully. Most were so old the dyes and inks had faded; there were deeds and agreements, land-holdings, some old king-lists that made Skapti mutter bitterly.

'These should be re-copied.' He held one up to the light. 'This is a family list of the Wulfings; it goes back ten generations.'

'But the poets know all those things, don't they?' Hakon said.

'Yes, passed from teacher to pupil. But there's always the chance they'll be lost. I never even knew these existed.'

'They were here before Gudrun's time,' Brochael said, 'but no-one seems to have looked at them for years. There don't seem to be many maps.'

They found land-holdings for dead farmers, agreements swearing the end of blood-feuds, promises of weregild, tributes and taxes from southland kings none of them had ever heard of. There were poems and fragments and even a piece of deerskin inscribed with tiny red runes that Jessa handed to Kari. 'What do you think that is?'

'It's a spell,' he said, staring at it in surprise.

'What for?'

'I don't know. I can't read it. But I can feel the power in it, faintly.'

Skapti took it off him and bent his long nose over it. 'It's old. It's for making a goat give more milk.'

'Useful,' Jessa remarked, drily.

'There are others.' Brochael gathered a great sheaf out of the bottom of the chest. 'As you say, not of much use to us.'

'This might be.' Hakon was sitting with something open on his knee. He lifted it onto the table and spread it out.

It was a map, drawn on ancient sealskin, dried out and fragile. The corners were charred as if it had been once dragged from some fire. Jessa leaned forward, curious.

Marked at the bottom of the map was the jagged coastline of the Cold Sea, with the long narrow fjords they all knew so well reaching upwards into the land. The Jarlshold was clearly shown, a tiny cross with the rune J underneath. All the ports on the coast – Ost, Trond, Wormshead, Hollfara – had their names under them, and rivers and larger lakes were marked

27

with blue lines. Drawn in red dye was the old giant's road that led from the Jarlshold to Thrasirshall, and branching off from it another red line led north, straight up to the top of the map.

'What's that?' Jessa asked, putting her finger on it.

'It looks like another road,' Hakon said.

Brochael nodded. 'It is. I know where it begins, but like most of the giant-road it's a ruin, lost under forests. Here and there are stone-built sections, poking through the snow. I've never travelled it. I don't know anyone who has.'

'Now's your chance,' Hakon said wistfully. 'You could follow it north.'

Jessa looked at him sidelong. He was scratching his cheek with his thumbnail and looking strangely at the map; almost a hungry look. She could guess why. Hakon had been a thrall for most of his life; a slave on a greasy little hold, and had never been able to leave it. Now he was free. But he was also Wulfgar's man, one of his war-band. And if Wulfgar wasn't going . . .

Sadly she turned back to the map. The road ran north, clearly marked. Mountains and lakes and a large river were shown, but the further north it went the more empty the map became, until there was nothing but the road, as if whoever had drawn it had no knowledge of what lay up there lost under the snows.

Or perhaps he had heard stories. For at the very top of the map, right across the sealskin, was a great black slash, as if some enormous chasm or crevasse opened there, and the road ran right to its edge, or into it. Some words were scrawled nearby, and Skapti read them out.

28

'The end of the road is unknown.'

The black chasm also had a word in it, written loosely and untidily.

Ginnungagap.

They stared at it in silence. Then Brochael looked up.

'What do the stories say?'

'You know what they say.'

'Remind us. Earn your keep.'

Skapti linked his long fingers together and flexed them. 'Ginnungagap is a howling emptiness,' he said simply. 'It's the place where the sky comes down to meet the earth. It's a great chasm that encircles the earth – here in the north its edges are heavy with ice; an eternal wind roars out of it, night and day. Long ago, they say, there was only the Gap. Then a creature crawled out of it, a frost-giant, called Ymir. The gods killed him. From his body they made Middle-earth; the rocks from his bones, the stones from his teeth. His skull is the blue sky – four dwarves sit at the corners to hold it up. So the poets say. But one thing is sure, the Gap is still there.' He was silent a moment, then added some lines, quietly.

'When Ymir lived, long ago,
Was no sand or sea, no surging waves.
Nowhere was there earth or heaven above,
But a grinning gap, and grass nowhere.'

'So what's beyond it?' Jessa said.

He stared at her in surprise. 'Nothing. That's what they say. Nothing. It's the end.'

The thought of it silenced them; the frozen wastes of snow, the howling winter blackness of the world's

29

brink. Jessa brought her mind back to the warm room with an effort.

'But everyone says the White People live beyond the world's end. And they come here, from time to time, so . . .'

'I don't know!' Skapti said, exasperated. 'I'm a mere songster. A lackwit. A plucker of strings. How should I know? Perhaps there are worlds beyond this. No-one has ever tried it and come back, that's the truth.'

She tapped the map, its worn mountains and half-erased rivers. 'Then we'll be the first.'

'Well spoken, Jessa.'

Wulfgar stood in the doorway, his face flushed from the wind, his eyes bright. He came in, brushing the dust from his hair, then tugged off his coat and threw it at Brochael. 'You will. We'll make sure of that. This expedition will come back because none like it will ever have set out before. Sorcery, guile, strength, cleverness. You four have all those things. But I'd like to send one more thing with you. A sword.'

They looked at him, uncertain, but he smiled at them, his old lazy smile. 'No, not me. You were right about that.' Sitting down, he leaned back in the chair, gripping the arms. 'I am the Jarl,' he said, proudly, and a little sadly, 'and I won't desert my people. No, I want you to take Hakon. You'll need another swordsman.'

Amazed, Hakon gaped at him. 'But I'm not . . . I mean I've been training hard, but my hand is still not as . . .'

Wulfgar leaned forward. 'Hakon Emptyhand,

30

you'll do as your lord tells you. Someone has to keep an eye on Jessa.'

She glared at him, then laughed. 'Five then.'

'Five. And a better five I couldn't have. Because it all depends on you,' he added softly. 'Signi's life. All of it.' He rubbed his hair again. 'I don't know what I'll do when you're all gone.'

In the silence Kari caught her glance. He was watching Wulfgar apprehensively, as if there was something else he had not told him, but when he saw her looking he smiled, and shook his head. She felt awkward. For a moment she had been wondering if Kari had changed Wulfgar's mind for him.

5

Silence I ask of the sacred folk.

Jessa walked thoughtfully between the houses, through the noise and bustle of preparation. Outwardly the hold seemed to be back to normal after the bewildering spell-storm; the smiths hammered, the fishing boats were out, women gossiped and spun wool in the sun.

And yet she had begun to realize that the dreams were still here.

Twice in the night she had woken from strange, tangled visions. Not only that, but the weather was cold. Too cold. Since midsummer a keen wind had whistled round the hold continuously; made draughts in all the rooms and corridors, moving tapestries, banging doors and shutters, touching the back of her neck like cold fingers.

She went in, past the sacks that were being packed with food, and up the stairs. Skapti was coming down, carrying the kantele, his precious instrument, well-wrapped.

'You're taking that, then?' she asked, passing him.

'Some of us have to work, Jessa.'

They were to leave in two days. Wulfgar and ten of his men were riding with them to the borders of the land, to the giant road. He'd insisted on that. As

32

she ran up the stairs she clenched her fingers in her pockets, puzzled at how cold they were. Then she tapped on the door.

A woman opened it.

'Any change?' Jessa whispered.

Fulla shook her head. She was Signi's step-mother, an elderly woman. Her iron-grey hair was bound in long braids; her dress hung with ivory charms. She let Jessa in, and they both stood by the silken hangings.

Signi lay unmoving, her beautiful corn-gold hair brushed smooth. Her eyes were open, blue and clear and empty.

Jessa picked up the cold fingers. 'Hear me, Signi,' she said.

Nothing. No flicker, no turn of the head.

Slowly Jessa laid the limp hand down. 'She seems cold.'

'She is. The woman bent to touch the girl's forehead. 'And I'm sure she's getting colder. I keep the fire well-stoked, but the room has a growing chill. I've told the Jarl. It worries me.'

Coming out, Jessa went back down the stairs. She was worried too, worried and restless. She went to the outside door and looked out. Wind caught her hair and whipped it up; the chill made her shiver. Something was wrong here. She looked around carefully, noticing other things. Most of the hens were inside, and very quiet. Up on the fellside the goats were huddled together, in the shelter of boulders and tall trees. And now she came to realize it, there were no birds about the hold. None but Kari's ravens, hunched up on the hall-roof like black carvings.

On impulse, she ran between the houses and up the hillside and knelt, looking closely. The grass looked shrivelled. Small flowers of tormentil and thrift, bright yellow and pink two days ago, were brown wet stems. She picked one; it was rotten down to the heart, the leaves a blackening clot. Rolling it in her fingers she stood, looking over the fellside.

All the flowers were gone. Gudrun's unseasonal frost had seared the land here, though far off, well up the fjordshore, it was still midsummer, the soft colours flaunting in the meadows. And there were no new green shoots. The raw wind flapped and gusted, but only in the hold; in bewilderment she stared up at the trees behind her; the forest was still, its dark fringe unmoving.

She ran back down, frowning.

Kari was sitting in his room with Hakon. As she came in she saw that he was carving another small bone circle with deft, skilful cuts.

'Why didn't you tell me?' she demanded.

Kari's knife paused in mid-air.

'Tell you what?' Hakon asked in surprise.

'He knows.' She sat down, between them. 'It's still here, isn't it? Why didn't you tell us?'

Kari put the knife down on the bench and looked at it bleakly. 'Keep your voice down, Jessa. If the holders know they might panic.'

Hakon had stopped burnishing his sword. 'What's still here?'

'The spell. Whatever Gudrun sent.'

'How did you find out?' Kari asked quietly.

'The flowers.' She laid them on the bench. 'The weather. The wind.'

'It's not wind.' Kari picked up the ring of bone and turned it over. 'Those are dreams, moving around us.'

'Can you see them?' Hakon asked, horrified.

34

Kari looked at him sideways. 'I should have been ready for her!' he said, suddenly bitter. 'Since she sent the rune-creature, last year, I've been gathering watchers round the hold. But she was too sudden, too fierce.'

'Watchers?'

Kari looked at him. 'Ghosts,' he said.

Hakon paled.

Kari clenched his fingers on the bone disc. 'You're right, Jessa, the rune-spell is still here. It won't go. I can see it from the corners of my eyes; a coldness growing in the hold. It's wrapped around Signi, but she was just the first. It will spread, an icy sleep, and one by one, without warning, they'll all fall into it, their souls slipping away from them. Winter will close in. The fjord will freeze, the fires go out. Farmers, fishermen, thralls, they'll all lie down and the ice will cover them slowly, month by month. Even the beasts. She's wrapped the hold in its own dreams, and there's almost nothing I can do about it.'

'Almost?'

He flipped the bone ring. 'I have an idea. But most of all we have to find Signi.'

'That's exactly what Gudrun wants.'

'Of course it is.'

They sat silent, feeling he had spoken prophecy; like a shaman reading the future. Perplexed, Hakon rubbed the dragons on his sword. 'Have you told Wulfgar this?'

'Yesterday. As soon as I was sure. It's another reason he has to stay.'

'But why should any of them stay?' Jessa said suddenly. 'Why not clear everyone out of the hold . . .?'

His look silenced her. 'No-one can escape their dreams, Jessa. We five who go, I can protect. That's all.'

'And those left?'

He spun the bone ring on the bench. 'This.'

She picked it up and turned it over. 'What is it?'

The smooth white surface was carved with small running lines. They seemed to move before her eyes, as if they rippled. He took it from her, quickly. 'It's their defence . . .'

A babble of noise outside interrupted him; raised, urgent voices. Jessa jumped up and went to the window. After a second she said, 'Come and see this.'

Hakon came behind her; Kari at her shoulder.

Below them, a man was bent over in the mud; a small crowd gathering anxiously round him. He was shouting, his face white and desperate. As Wulfgar and Skapti came running up the crowd moved back a little, and Jessa saw a small boy lying on the ground, curled up as if he was asleep. A handful of grain spilled from his closed fist; the hens still pecked at it, hungrily.

'The children,' Kari whispered. 'They'll be the first.'

'Come on!' She pushed past him, ran down the stairs and out, and they both followed her, without a word. The crowd fell silent as Kari made his way in beside Wulfgar.

'Has it started already?' the Jarl murmured.

Kari touched the boy's forehead; the father glared, as if he would have pushed him away but dared not. For a moment Kari was still, his face remote, his colourless eyes watching the sleeping child. Then he looked at Wulfgar, and nodded.

36

'What's the matter with him?' the father yelled.

The Jarl caught him by the arm. 'Summon your courage, Gunnar. The boy is asleep, that's all. Take him home and put him to bed; I'll send you some help.'

Watching him go he said, 'It's beginning, then.'

The door to the hall slammed wide, startling them all; inside they saw the tapestries billowing in the dream-wind. A tiny flake of snow, no bigger than a shieldnail, sailed down and settled on Jessa's sleeve. It did not melt for a long time.

'Find Brochael,' Wulfgar said grimly. 'Tell him to get the men ready. We leave in the morning.'

Then he turned back and looked at Kari. 'You said this will spread. How far?'

'The hold first. It's already here – I can't stop that. Afterwards, over the whole realm.'

'Then we need some way to contain it, Kari. Anything.'

Kari nodded, slowly. 'I'll do what I can.'

6

Wider and wider through all worlds I see.

Late in the night Brochael woke up and turned in the cramped sleeping-booth. It was too small for him, as they usually were, but this time he was glad of the discomfort, because the strange dream of the cell had come to him again, and the memory of it disturbed him.

After a moment he sat up, with a mutter of irritation. It was cold in the stone room; the fire must have gone out.

He dragged the great bearskin from the bed, swung it round himself, and padded over the floor, scratching his tousled red hair. The brazier held a low glimmer of peats, and as he dropped new ones in, the light darkened even more, making the room a huddle of cold shadows. Still, it would blaze up eventually and last till morning.

He watched it sleepily for a moment, his mind avoiding the echoes of the dream. Gudrun's sorcery still lurked here. It was not often that he thought about her – he hated the woman for what she had done to her son. Apart from Kari only he, Brochael, knew the full evil of that. And he feared her. As for Kari . . . all at once he realized how quietly the boy was sleeping, and turned, quickly.

38

The bed was empty.

For a moment, rigid, Brochael stared at it. Then he shook his head, dragged the bench up to the warmth and sat down, leaning back against the wall. The alarm that had flared in him for a second died down – he knew Kari well enough. The boy had strange gifts, and they drove him strangely. Often at home, in Thrasirshall, he would walk the snowfields and forests all night, the ravens flapping above him. Brochael knew he spoke to ghosts and wraiths and invisible things out there; things he could tell no-one else about. He tugged the bearskin tight on his broad back. Wherever Kari was, it was his own realm. He was skilful there.

Under the oak tree at the edge of the wood Kari was digging; making a small pit with his knife in the moist soil under the leafdrift. Around him the night was silent; the wood a dank, rustling mass of darkness, rich with the smell of moss and wood-rot.

When the hole was deep enough he took a pouch from his belt, felt about inside for one of the small bone counters, and dropped it in.

'The last?' a voice croaked above him.

'Two more.' He straightened, stamping the soil down quickly, rubbing it from his hands. 'One more to close the ring. Near the shore, somewhere.'

The moon glinted on his hair and face as he pushed through the tangle of bush and underbrush. Rowan saplings sprouted here at the wood's edge; thorn and hazel and great fronds of bracken between them, chest-high. In the dappled silver light fat stems cracked and snapped under his feet. He struggled through, noticing the frosted crisp ends of the leaves, already dying. About him the night whispered; the dream-wind brought him voices and murmurs and crystals of snow; two dark shapes drifted above him from tree to tree.

Then he paused, and looked back.

A small boy stood in the wood, watching him. Caught in the moonlight the child seemed faint, pale as bone. Kari took a step towards him; the boy backed away. Dirty tearstains smeared his face.

'You're the Snow-walker,' he muttered.

'I won't hurt you.'

The boy looked up, bewildered, at the high, rustling trees.

Finally he came forward. His hand reached out to Kari's sleeve. 'I can't get back in,' he whispered. 'I can't. And none of them can see me any more. No-one talks to me but you. Father tells me to wake up but I can't. I'm outside.'

Kari crouched in the mud beside him. 'I know that,' he said gently. 'Your name is Einar Gunnarsson, isn't it?'

The boy nodded, rubbing his face. 'I was feeding the hens . . .'

'You will get back,' Kari said urgently, 'but I don't know when.'

'My father keeps calling me! And I'm cold.' He shuddered, and looked round. 'And the others frighten me.'

'Others?' Kari clenched his fingers. 'People you know? People from the hold?'

'No. Shadow-people. I don't know them. They're worn thin, like ghosts. And there are wolves that flicker between me and the moon. Ships out on the water . . .'

'Have you seen a girl?' Kari asked quickly. 'Signi. You remember her?'

'She fell asleep.'

'That's right.'

The boy shook his head. He took a step back, through a trunk of birch. 'Has that happened to me? Am I dreaming this? I want to get out of the dream. I want to go home.' Suddenly he turned and ran down among the trees to the hold, sobbing. Kari watched him go, fading to a glimmer of moonlight. Then he dropped his head and stared in despair at the leaflitter on the ground. His silver hair hung still.

'Not your fault,' a dark voice said.

'In a way it is,' he said, without looking up. 'She wants me. I should have gone with her when she asked. I knew she would never leave them alone.'

He jerked up and pushed his way through and out of the wood, the two birds swooping above him, then ran down to the shore, where the black water lapped silently.

In the shingle he gouged another hole and dropped a bone-disc in, then covered it with tiny stones and sand. A large boulder lay nearby; he tried to shift it but couldn't. 'Help me,' he muttered.

They came, one on each side of him, tall, dark men, their long taloned fingers tight on the rock. Together they dragged it over the buried talisman. Then Kari straightened, wearily.

'That's it.'

He looked back, and saw the ring he had made around the hold; felt its power throb and tighten. The dream-spell was held inside; none of it could escape. 'The last should be left in the hall. A secret guardian over the sleepers.'

He walked quickly through the sleeping hold, by shapes he knew, that lurked at the corners of the houses. Coming to the hall he went straight past the watchman, opening the door and letting himself in softly, blanking the man's mind and releasing it as soon as he was inside. The man scratched his hair, seeing nothing; the dog at his feet watched, silently.

In the hall, Kari moved between the sleeping warband to the rooftree. The ancient ash-trunk rose high over him, the snake-mark already half planed away by Wulfgar's thralls. Two raven shapes drifted after him through the high windows.

'Here,' he said quietly. 'This will be the place where the last of them gather. Whoever's still awake. This is the heart of the hold.'

He took something small from the pouch and held it up for a moment, the moonlight glinting on its brightness. Then he bent and found a small slit in the seamed trunk, and pushed the shining fragment well inside with his long fingers. 'Guard them,' he whispered. 'Till the time comes.'

For a moment he stood there, winding it with spells and runes of protection, filaments of hope. Then he looked up at the birds. 'I think you should stay too.'

One of them seemed to laugh, a harsh grating sound. 'We go with you Kari. What could we do here, with these sightless men?'

'They see well enough. Differently to us, that's all.' He pushed his hair away wearily. 'Now I've done all I can for them. Her power is here already though. Nothing can change that.'

As he said it the tapestries rippled with a faint breeze. Some of the sleeping men turned uneasily in their fleeces and wraps. He watched them for a

42

moment, tasting their dreams, then went quietly upstairs.

Brochael sat up as the door opened, his face a warm glow.

'All done?' he asked, quietly.

Kari sat on the end of the bench and tugged his boots off.

'All done,' he said.

They looked at each other, a flicker of understanding.

In the cold morning Jessa tied her bundle more firmly to the pack-horse and swung herself up onto her own pony.

'Yes, but why not go by sea? At least to start with.'

Skapti was picking at the upturned hoof of his horse with careful fingers. 'Because of the ice.' He put the beast's leg down and gave it an encouraging slap. Then he looked at her across the saddle. 'If you sail around the coast, beyond Trond, beyond all the fjords, the coast starts to turn north, yes, but after a week or so, even in summer, you reach the ice. I've spoken to a few men who've tried it. Great floating bergs of ice. And if you manage to avoid them and sail on, the ice becomes thicker; smashed plates of it, jagged and sharp. The winter's teeth. Many ships have been eaten by them. Beyond that they say, you reach a wall of ice, unbroken, higher than the Jarlshall. No-one has ever crossed that.'

Jessa laughed. 'I'm convinced.'

'Good.' He swung himself up. 'Are you all armed, Jessa Two-knives?'

'All armed.'

She watched Kari come down the steps in his dark

43

coat. He looked bone-pale in the wan light, and tired, as if he had not slept. Brochael was behind him, the huge axe under one arm.

They climbed up onto their horses and waited, the courtyard an agitated clatter of hooves, whinneying, shouts for those who were missing. A drum beat quietly from the corner of the hall; an old man in a shaman's coat of feathers chanted luck-songs and charms in a quavering voice.

Hakon came running round the corner with a bundle falling from his back and the precious sword under his arm; he fastened them both hastily onto the restless horse. His friends from the war-band mocked him, and he got flustered and did the straps up wrongly. Watching him, Jessa saw how he had grown since he had been here. As a thrall he had been thin – now his arms were strong, his eyes quick from long sword-practice with Wulfgar's men. As he scrambled up she said, 'We thought you weren't coming.'

He grinned at her. 'Jessa, you won't get rid of me. This is my first real adventure, my first journey! I've dreamed of this for a long time.'

She nodded, thinking that it was dreams they were escaping from. He was the only one who seemed really happy. Wulfgar, on his black horse, looked morosely round. Then he nodded to Brochael. 'We're all here.'

And he turned the horse and led the company out of the hold, riding proudly between the houses, past the ships on the fjord, scattering chickens and a bleating, long-eared goat. The holders watched them go, muted and sombre; only the children waved and shouted, dancing alongside.

Jessa turned in the saddle and waved back to them, sadly. She tried not to think about whether she would ever see them again.

Or they her.

She knew she was going too far to come back unchanged.

45

7

Men tread Hel's road.

They rode north, along the fjordshore. The path was broad, well-used; it ran through the fringes of the woods and out over the wide grazing land of the Jarlsholders.

All through that first day the sun warmed the riders, and quiet warbles of birdsong filled the branches about them. Bees and maybugs and long, glinting dragonflies hummed over the shallows of the still water; occasionally a fish snapped upwards, sending a plop of tiny ripples racing to the shore.

Twice they passed fishermen, out on the blue water in their flimsy craft, who paused over their nets and watched the cavalcade pass, curious. On the fellsides goats and the long-haired sheep lifted their heads and stared unmoving. This was rich pastureland, owned by men who were respected, Wulfgar's firmest supporters. And it was still midsummer here, the air tinged with the scents of the innumerable flowers, so that the horses waded in clouds of blown seed and spindrift, and the crushed, sharp scents of watermint and warm thyme.

If it could all be this easy, Jessa thought, struggling out of her coat and laying it across the horse in front of her. She laughed at Skapti; day-dreaming, he had almost jerked from his horse as it stumbled.

Far ahead, Wulfgar rode with Kari. They were talking, close together. Looking back she saw Brochael joking with the men, they all roared with laughter. Hakon was just behind her.

'He's telling them horrible stories,' he muttered. 'I don't think you should listen.'

Jessa grinned. 'I expect I told him most of them.'

She laughed at his shocked look, then watched a line of swans skitter down on the rippling water. 'It's easy to forget, out here.'

'Forget?'

'Signi. And the rest.'

He nodded, brushing the swinging leaves away from his face. 'I can't understand . . . how can her soul be gone?'

'Kari says so. He knows about these things.'

'And what's to stop Gudrun doing that to us – to any of us?'

She looked at him. 'Only Kari, I suppose.'

Uneasy, he said, 'It makes me feel useless. I'm only a swordsman, not even a very good one. Sorcery makes me shiver. Why did Wulfgar send me?'

For a moment she said nothing. Then she shook her head. 'Kari needs us, just as we need him. Maybe more. Wulfgar knows that.' Seeing his worried look she laughed. 'Anyway, maybe the Jarl wanted to get rid of you for a while.'

He laughed with her, quietly.

Late in the afternoon, with the long blue twilight barely beginning, the fjord had narrowed to a thin strip of water, the meadows on the other side drawn close. They stayed that night at a hold called

47

Audsstead, the woman Aud riding out with her sons to meet them. Jessa went to bed early, yawning, leaving the talk and laughter in the great hall.

Next day the land began to change. They rode uphill now, and inland. The slopes were steeper, the grass short and sheep-nibbled, studded with boulders that broke the turf as if they were the land's bones, under its green skin. Here and there the slopes were boggy; the horses' hooves sank deep into soft peat; masses of lichen and bright moss matting the treacherous ground.

At last they stopped to eat, high above the fjord. Looking down, Jessa thought the sliver of water was a flooded crack in the land; as if the hills floated above reflections of sky and pale, passing clouds.

Brochael nudged her arm. 'All well?'

'Just daydreaming.' She snuggled up against him. 'How long before we reach the road?'

He shrugged. 'We're on it, Jessa, more or less. Only a path is left here, no masonry. We go over this hill ahead and down into a place called Thorirsdale. Beyond that, in the forest somewhere, the road divides. That's as far as Wulfgar will come. From then on, we're on our own.'

She was silent for a moment. 'Will we get there today?'

'Tomorrow. Tonight we'll stay at Thorirstead. I know Ulf. He used to beat me at wrestling, when we were boys.'

Amazed, Jessa looked up at him. 'You mean he's bigger than you!'

'He's a giant. He likes to boast he's the descendant of those who built the road. I believe him, for one.'

'I hope not!' Looking round she said. 'Where's Kari?'

'Off with the ravens.'

There was the hint of something odd in his voice but she had no time to pin it down; Wulfgar was telling everyone to mount up. He came and stood looking down at them.

'Comfortable?'

Jessa grinned. 'Very.'

He smiled, but briefly, and she knew the thought of Signi was weighing on him, and the dread of what he might find when he went back. She scrambled up, wishing she hadn't said anything.

'Where's Kari?' he asked Brochael.

'About.'

'We'd better find him.'

'There's no need.' Brochael heaved his bag up onto the horse and fiddled with the saddle-straps. 'He'll come. He'll know we're waiting.'

Wulfgar shook his head as Kari came over the brow of the hill just then and waved at them, the birds wheeling joyously round his head.

'Sometimes I wonder if there's anything he can't do.'

'He can't steal souls,' Brochael muttered. 'At least, not yet.'

When they rode over the hill-top they saw before them the green plenty of Thorirsdale; a wide valley, its tiny silver streams gushing down noisily. This end was pastureland, and they could see the smoke from the farmstead rising near the narrow river. Beyond that the land rose again to deep woods, dark against the sky.

As they rode into the valley the light lessened; the shoulders of the hills rose about them. Down here the air was warm and hushed, the last of the evening birdsong fading over the fields. By the time they neared the hold the purple half-night had begun, and the weak sun was lost behind the hills.

There was a long low building which looked like the farmhouse, roofed in green turf to keep in the warmth. Smoke rose from a hearth-hole near its centre; Jessa smelt its sharpness. Other buildings clustered round it; barns and byres, all very quiet and dark under the rising moon.

The horses' hooves crunched down the narrow track.

'Perhaps they're all asleep,' Jessa said.

'Not Ulf,' Brochael muttered.

A dog barked ahead, then another. After a moment a slot opened in the dark house; light and smoke and cooking smells streamed out. The great bulk of a man clogged the doorway; then he strode out, others behind him.

'Who have I to welcome at this time of night?'

He glanced out at the riders through the eerie night-mist, taking them in quickly, their numbers and strength; a tall, heavy man, his hair shaved close, a long sword held easily in his hand.

Wulfgar dismounted. 'Me, Ulf Thorirsson.'

'Jarl!' The holder turned, surprised. 'What's happened?' he asked quickly, seeing Wulfgar's face. 'What's wrong?'

'Plenty,' Wulfgar said, grimly. 'But it'll keep until we're inside.'

Ulf nodded, passing his sword back to a thrall. 'My house is honoured. In now, all of you. My men will see to the animals.' He swept round and collided with Brochael, who had been standing close behind him. Half-way off her horse Jessa giggled at the look on his face, half amazement, half delight.

'Brochael?' he breathed.

'Come for a re-match, Ulf.' Brochael folded his arms looked his old friend up and down. 'You've been overeating. Running to fat.'

Ulf grinned. 'There's been no-one here to challenge me.'

'Until now.'

They gripped hands, and Ulf slapped Brochael with a palm that would have made most men crumple. 'It's good to see you,' he said warmly.

The hall was small, and heavy with smoke. Food was cooked here over the central hearth. The women of the farm were thrown into cold terror by the sight of Jarl and all his war-band descending on them out of the night, until Ulf's wife, a tall, gaunt woman called Helga, gave quiet, efficient orders.

The high table was cleared; Wulfgar sat in the centre, his friends on each side of him, Kari next to Jessa. She knew he was uneasy. Once the excitement of their arrival had died down the people of the hold were only interested in him. They stared frankly, like animals, until he looked up, and then their eyes slid away.

'Centre of attention,' Jessa whispered.

He nodded, silent.

She trimmed the meat with her knife. 'You must be getting used to it.'

'You never do.' He picked listlessly at his food.

'It's not the way they look, but what they feel. Fear. Gudrun's shadow.'

There was no denying that, she thought. In the silence that followed, she began to listen to Wulfgar. He was explaining what had happened at the Jarlshold, and Ulf was listening, gravely. Brochael had been right; this man was enormous, a head higher than anyone else, even Skapti, his neck thick as a sapling. The coarse wool of his shirt strained over his broad back. Jessa saw that the chair he sat in was huge and old, its legs carved like wolves, their backs arched to bear his weight.

'Will it spread?' Ulf said urgently. 'If the whole of the Jarlshold falls into the witch-spell, what's to stop it spreading out here?'

Wulfgar looked at Kari.

Kari spoke quietly. 'It won't leave the Jarlshold. I've made a binding-ring of bone. The dream-spell is trapped inside. It won't spread, as long as the people stay within.'

'What sort of ring?' Ulf asked, curiously. He stared down at Kari's thin face shrewdly, without fear. 'Sorcery, is this?'

'You could call it that.'

'And you trust it, Jarl?'

Wulfgar smiled, slowly. 'I trust it.'

'Then that's good enough for me. But what about the people in the hold?'

Wulfgar's expression hardened. 'We'll stay. That's the choice we've had to make.' Then as if to forget, he reached out a lazy hand for more wine, and leaned back. 'This is a fine hall, Ulf.'

'My father built it. Now there was a big man, bigger even than me.' He scratched his stubbly beard.

'Indeed he was,' Brochael passed the wine. 'They say he once carried a stray reindeer home, two days' journey. Is that true?'

Ulf nodded, proudly. 'Thorir Giant-blood, they called him.'

'Tell us about the road,' Wulfgar said.

The huge man sat still, the firelight warming his face. Behind him his massive shadow darkened the hung shields.

'There's not much known about it. All the stories of the giants are almost forgotten; even who they were. Your friend here would know more about that than me.'

Skapti nodded, wryly.

'But the road,' Ulf went on, 'is real enough. It goes north. They say it runs even to the edge of the world, to a country where the snow falls all night and all day, and where in winter the sun never rises. No-one has ever travelled a week's journey along it, to my knowledge, except Laiki.'

'Laiki?' Wulfgar murmured.

'An old man now.' Ulf stood up and roared, 'Thror! Fetch Laiki!' and sat down again. 'He went, in his younger days. He tells strange tales about it, and they get stranger year by year. I don't promise, Jarl, that any of them are true.'

The old man came up slowly. He was shrivelled, his hair white as wool, long and straggly. A thick fleece coat covered his body, and as he grasped the chair and lowered himself into it they saw his hand had two fingers missing; two stumps were left, long healed.

'Well, father, we hear you know something of the giant-road.' Wulfgar leaned forward and poured him a drink. 'My friends will be travelling that way. Can you tell us about it?'

The old man's weak blue eyes looked at them all. He seemed delighted, Jessa thought, to have such an audience.

'Once, I went that way.'

'Long ago?'

He wheezed out a laugh. 'Forty years or more, masters. Forty years. Two other men and I, we set out to find the road's end. We had learned there was amber up there in the north, and jet. We wanted wealth. Like all young men, we were fools.'

He smiled at Jessa, and put a cool hand on hers. 'Are you going on this journey?'

'Yes,' she said, quietly.

'Not just young men, then.' He shook his head. 'The road is paved at first, masters, whole and easy. After a while it becomes fragmented. It leads into a great forest, dark and deep. Ironwood, my friends called it, for a joke, but we were more than a week in that haunted ghost-ridden place, and all the time we heard the stir and passing of invisible spirits, as if a great army of men whispered about us in the dark. None of us slept. We walked day and night to leave that nightmare behind. The air became colder. One night we came to a great ruined hall, deep in the wood. We were exhausted, and slept, and when we woke one of my friends had gone. We never found him.'

He gazed round at them, soberly.

'After the wood, the ice. We struggled on, but our food was gone and our hearts were failing. Then wolves came. Alric was killed, and the horses that we hadn't yet eaten ran off. I wandered alone in the empty land, a place of glaciers, wide snowplains where the icy winds roared all night. I was lost there, starved and delirious. I do not remember, masters, how I got back through the wood. Sometimes it seems to me that I saw terrible sights, things I can't piece together; a great city in a lake, a bridge that rose up to the stars, but I cannot tell if these things were real or a delirium.' He paused, sighing. 'All I do know, is that I came to myself in a shieling north of here, nursed back to health by a shepherd. For two weeks I had lain there, he said, babbling the nightmares of the wood.'

He held up his hand. 'And these fingers were gone. Bitten off, the good man thought. And to this day I do not know what happened to me.'

He looked round at them all. 'If your journey is not urgent, masters, take my advice. Turn back. That is no country for mortals.'

They were silent a moment.

Then Brochael shook his head. 'Lives depend on it, old man. We've no choice.'

8

I tell of giants from times forgotten,
Those who fed me in former days.

The road was floored with great slabs, powdered with grey and green overlapping lichens. Here and there saplings had sprouted up through the gaps between stones, and bushes of thorn and rowan, but the way was still surprisingly easy to follow, leading downhill among the light-barred glades of trees.

Jessa sat herself down on the edge of it and looked closely at the giants' handiwork. The slabs had been squared and laid close, each one flat and slotted in neatly to its neighbour. It would take many men and horses to lift even a few. No wonder people thought of giants.

'Are there such things?' she asked aloud.

'Indeed there are. Or there were.' Skapti drew his long knees up. 'Once, at Hollfara, I saw a merchant selling bones. Huge bones they were, immense, Jessa, bigger than any man or animal, except the great serpent that winds around the earth. What else could they be but giants' bones?'

She touched the amulet at her neck, lightly. 'Then I hope we don't meet any! Ulf's big enough.'

She watched him saying goodbye to Brochael.

'Time to go.'

Reluctantly, the skald got up after her.

Wulfgar lifted her onto her horse and stood there while Hakon and Brochael mounted. Kari was already waiting, the ravens silent on a branch above him. Wulfgar looked at them all. 'It hurts me bitterly to let you all go.' He glanced at Skapti. 'Especially you.'

Skapti gave a lop-sided smile. 'You can get yourself a better poet. You've always wanted to.'

'There is no better poet.' He put a hand on Skapti's shoulder. 'If you don't come back, and I haven't been caught in the witch-spell, then I'll come looking for you. One day.'

Skapti nodded. He climbed up onto the long-maned horse and the five of them looked at each other, silent among the crowd of men.

'Good luck,' Wulfgar said simply. He glanced at Kari. 'There are no others but you who could do this. Let the gods watch you.'

'And you,' Brochael rumbled.

'Goodbye, Wulfgar,' Jessa said sadly. She turned her horse and rode out quickly over the grey stones, the others following, Hakon tugging the long rein of the packhorse.

They clattered down the slope, between the sprouting trees. When Jessa looked back she saw Wulfgar standing at the top, arms folded, watching them. He raised a hand. Then the bushes hid him, and all the men with him.

They were alone.

It was a silent journey, that descent of the ancient road.

None of them wanted to talk, and there was no

sense of danger on them, so they rode in a long, straggling line, picking their way over the broken paving.

The road led down and up, winding over low hills, its grey line visible sometimes far ahead. Late in the day they rode over a high moor, with the grey scatter of broken paving stretching in front of them, mosses and peat spreading out over it, as if the land was drawing it back.

Hakon slowed his horse. 'What's that?'

On the horizon, a gaunt pillar stood stark against the cloudy sky.

'Dead tree,' Brochael suggested.

'Too straight.' Skapti narrowed his eyes. 'A rock, maybe.'

Cautiously, they rode towards it. As they came close they saw that he was right, but that this rock too had been shaped, heaved upright. Sliced deep into its surface was a carving of three wolves, tangled together, their jaws agape. Behind them, his great hands reining them in, stood a huge man, his head roughly shaped, his eyes looking fiercely out. Unfamiliar words were carved at his feet.

'Can you read it?' Jessa asked Skapti.

The skald dismounted and went over to the stone, reaching up and fingering the carving thoughtfully. 'No. These are no runes I know. And it's old, Jessa. Centuries.'

'It could be a gravestone,' Hakon said, uneasily.

'It could. But I think it's a marker of territory. Or was.'

'Giants?' Brochael wondered.

Skapti shrugged, and climbed back onto his horse. 'Maybe. But long ago.'

Jessa looked at Kari. He was gazing up at the stone, his eyes strangely distant. For a moment she thought he was listening to some sound, straining to catch it, but when he saw her looking he said nothing.

They went on, but after that silent warning a sense of foreboding seemed to fall on them; they rode together now, and more warily.

Slowly the long day died, but still they travelled, not knowing where to stop. Finally, in a small copse of birch by the roadside, they saw the rise of a thatched roof.

Brochael drew rein. 'I'll go and see,' he said. 'Skapti, come too. The rest of you, wait here.'

But the ravens had come karking down about Kari in a flutter of noise; they perched on the grey stones, walking and pecking over them.

'They say it's empty,' Kari said.

Brochael glared at him. 'Are you sure?'

'So they say.'

Everyone stared at the birds, but they knew better than to doubt him. Brochael urged his horse off the road. 'This is going to be a very strange expedition,' he muttered.

It was an old shepherd's hut, long deserted. Trees had sprouted in the doorway, and the walls had gaping holes, but the roof was more or less intact, and the floor seemed dry.

They hacked their way in and soon had a fire lit; Hakon and Jessa rubbed the horses down and let them graze, tied to a long rope.

'What about wolves?' Hakon said, nervously.

Jessa gathered up her pack. 'We'll hear them. And we can't take the beasts in with us, can we?'

'I suppose not,' he said, grinning.

59

Later, as they ate around the fire, Brochael brought out the map. He opened it, the waxed seal-skin crackling under his fingers, and spread it out on his coat. 'We should add to this, as we go. That stone, for instance.'

'No ink.' Jessa swallowed a mouthful of cheese too quickly.

'No.' He scowled.

'Besides,' Hakon said, looking at the parchment closely, 'maybe the stone we saw is this.' He put his finger on the faint ghost of a mark to the left of the red line; it was so worn it had almost gone, but now they looked closely it could once have been a rough suggestion of the stone, its carvings reduced to squiggles.

'So whoever made it got this far,' Skapti said dryly. 'That cheers me.'

'This hut,' Jessa waved her knife around, 'could be the hut the old man talked about. It must have belonged to Ulf's people once. It's too small for giants.'

The fire crackled and spat over the damp kindling. Outside, the night was still, and through the doorway they could see the stars, faint and pale.

'It's colder up here,' Hakon muttered.

'It'll get colder all the time.' Brochael tapped the map. 'This will be the forest.'

Tiny scratched trees were massed about the red line of the road. In the midst of them Jessa thought she saw something else; a faint rune, but she couldn't be sure.

'How long before we reach it?'

'A day. Two.' Brochael folded the skin quickly. 'Now. From now on we have someone awake always.

In turns. Kari first, then Jessa. We're out of the Jarlsrealm, and these are unknown lands. We should expect wolves, bears, outlaws maybe. Keep the fire going, Kari, but low. Not too much smoke.'

They rolled themselves in cloaks and blankets on the uncomfortable floor, and as Kari sat outside, leaning back against the wall, the gradual sounds of their breathing drifted out to him. Deep inside each of them he could feel the terror of his mother's spell, planted far down in their minds, ready to spread and trap them as it had trapped Signi and the boy. He knew each dream, and knew he couldn't destroy them, but only suppress them. So that each one would wake and forget.

Stretching out his legs he wrapped his dark cloak about him and looked up at the stars. They glinted, in their strange, spread patterns. Did the same stars shine over the land of the Snow-walkers? And was Gudrun looking up at them now? Though he ranged the night with his mind's whole power he could find no trace of her, or anything else either, in this strange empty land.

Except, far to the north, a sudden smudge of sound, that held him still for a moment, listening. A low murmur, like the beat of a drum. He stood up, and looked out through the still trees, but he knew already it was a ghost-sound, and not in this world.

'Did you hear that?'

The bird-shape above came down and stood beside him. 'We did. But far off.'

Together, they stared out over the unknown land.

9

Death is the portion of doomed men.

Two days later, early in the afternoon, they came to the edge of the wood.

For hours they had been riding through its outlying fringes, the scattered trees and sparse growths of hazel and birch, but now, coming down a steep hill-side, they saw the sudden thickening of the trees, a massing of greenery. Below them lay a mighty forest, its millions of treetops stirring in the soft breeze. It stretched far to the north, beyond sight into mist and low grey raincloud, as if somewhere it merged with the sky and dissolved there, at the edge of existence.

The road had dwindled to little more than a track, thin and muddy. It ran down among the trees and was swallowed.

Brochael ducked his head under a branch. 'Someone must still use it.'

Silent, they gathered beside him, letting the horses graze.

Jessa slid down and stretched, stiffly. 'So this is Ironwood. Easy to get lost in.'

Hakon took a long drink and wiped his mouth. 'I thought Ironwood was just a place in tales.'

'So it is,' Skapti said promptly, 'but all tales are true. They're just the way we struggle with the world.'

He folded his thin arms, looking out over the forest. 'The Ironwood of the stories is a very strange place. It lies far in the north-east. A giantess lives in its heart, with many troll-wives. She breeds sons, able to shape-shift into wolf-form. All the wolves of the world are descended from her. One day, they say, there will come an enormous wolf, called Hati, or Moongarm, who will strengthen himself by drinking the blood of all who die. Then he'll swallow the moon itself at the world's end, in the last conflict.' He raised a thin eyebrow. 'As the old man said, no place for mortals.'

'But this isn't that wood, is it?'

'Who knows. Perhaps every wood is that wood.'

'If it's not, the old man gave it a bitter name,' Brochael remarked. 'And stop teasing the boy, Skapti, or he'll be no good to any of us.'

The skald grinned. Hakon went red.

'But there are wolves.' Jessa got back on her horse. 'We've heard them.'

'And other beasts, I hope. Some fresh meat wouldn't come amiss.'

They picked their way down, carefully. The remaining stones of the road were cracked and treacherous, poking up here and there through mud and leaf-litter. As the riders passed silently into the wood they felt its rich scents wrap around them; tree-sap and fungi, crumbling bark, centuries of decay and growth. High above, the spindly branches of silver birch rustled, the sky blue and remote through the wind-blown boughs. Birds whistled here, flitting among the leaves, but gradually the wood became thicker and darker. The birches gave way to oaks, then a mass of evergreens; pine and spruce and fir, clogging the light. Soon the riders moved in a green gloom, silent except for the soft foot-falls of the horses.

Brochael rode ahead, with Kari and Jessa close behind. Skapti and Hakon came last, urging on the nervous pack-horse. The wood closed in. Branches hung down over the path, swishing back into their faces; far off, the dimness was split by shafts of sunlight, slanting here and there between the crowded trees.

After only a few minutes, Brochael stopped suddenly. Jessa's horse, always nervy, snorted and skittered sideways with fright, and she tugged its head around, trying not to back into Skapti.

Then she saw what had frightened it.

Skulls.

They were threaded, one above the other, hanging on long strings from the still branches; small skulls of birds and tiny animals – pine marten, stoat, rats, crows. Hundreds of them. In the faint breeze the bizarre hangings clicked and tapped against each other, the empty slits of their eyes turning. Half rotten, green with mould and lichen, beaks and teeth and bones swung in the dimness. Feathers were knotted into bundles among them, and the stink of decay hung under the trees.

'What is it?' Hakon whispered, appalled.

None of them answered him. The sudden smell of decay brought terror, numbing and cold. Centuries of superstition rose in their hearts, fear of sorcery, sacrifice, unknown rites. Small flies buzzed and whined about Jessa's face; she beat them off in disgust.

Then Kari nudged his horse forward. He rode in

under the long dangling lines of bone and caught one with his thin hands. Pulling it towards him he examined it carefully, the horse fidgeting beneath him.

His movement broke the stillness that held them. Jessa moved up beside him; the others came too, reluctantly.

'Look at this.' Kari's fingers slid the skulls apart; he touched carved circles of bone, each marked with runes; the same angular letters they had seen on the standing stone.

'What do they mean?' Brochael growled. He had his axe in his hand; he glanced around at the clinking curtain of death as if it made his skin crawl.

'Looks like a place of ritual,' Jessa muttered.

'Sacrifices?'

'Yes, but who left them,' Skapti murmured, 'and how long ago?'

Each of them kept their voices low; each of them noticed the human skulls, just a few, threaded here and there between the others.

Kari let the string of bones drop; it clicked and rattled and swung ominously to and fro. He was the only one of them who seemed unaffected by the grimness of the place. 'Some are old,' he said, thoughtfully, 'they've been here years. But that – that's new enough.'

It was the jawbone of a reindeer or some other grazing beast, snapped clean in half, impaled on the thorns of a bush. Strips of skin still hung from it. Around it, as if placed like offerings, were four small metal arrowheads, some black feathers, a broken bear's claw.

'This is sorcery,' Brochael muttered, backing suddenly. He gripped the thorshammer at his neck and looked at Kari as if there was a question he didn't know how to ask.

Kari answered it. 'I don't know for sure, but I think Jessa's right, in a way. The wood ahead of us is haunted by something. This is the barrier. Someone has made these offerings, built this curtain of power, hoping that whatever is in the wood can't pass it. I left something similar around the Jarlshold.'

Jessa looked at him in surprise but Brochael nodded. He looked worried. 'So what do we do?'

'We go on,' Skapti said, quietly.

'If the wood is haunted . . .'

'We have to go through, Brochael. Anything else would take too long.'

Each of them nodded, silent.

'Then we keep together, and all armed.'

'Let me go first,' Kari said.

'No!'

'Brochael,' Kari came up to him, his pale hair silvery in the dimness. 'I'm the best armed of all of you when it comes to things like this.'

For a moment Brochael said nothing. Then, with a grimace, he muttered, 'I know that.'

'So?'

'So watch my back.'

He turned his horse and led them out of the grove, between the bones that turned and glittered in the draught. Jessa pulled a wry face at Kari, and he smiled and shook his head. She for one was glad to get away from the horror of the skulls, but fear had fingered them now and they could not shake it off. The wood was full of shadows, sly movements, unease. Branches rustled, as if invisible watchers

66

touched them, and as the darkness grew to the dim blue of night a mist began to gather, waist-high, hanging between the dank boughs.

It became harder to keep to the path. Once, Brochael lost it, and they had to backtrack through an open stand of larches, bare of leaf below but black above. Skapti found a narrow track, but no-one could tell if it was the remains of the road or not. Suddenly, in the great silence, they knew they were lost.

Lost. Skapti felt the word crisp like a dead leaf in his mind.

Brochael swung himself down. 'Well, we had to stop somewhere; it may as well be here. We need daylight to see our way out of this.'

But Jessa thought that this was not a place they would have chosen. The wood had chosen it for them. It was open, with no real shelter among the trees; they built the fire near a mass of holly that might be some protection, but the kindling was damp and the mist put the flames out twice before Kari intervened and made them roar up and crackle.

It was a miserable night. They were short of water, and the damp glistened on their clothes and hair however close to the fire they crowded. They tried to keep up a conversation, and Skapti told stories, but in the silences between the words they were all listening.

The wood stirred and rustled around them. As night thickened their uneasiness grew. Once, a low thud of hooves in the distance made Hakon and Brochael leap up, weapons in hand, but the sound had gone; only the trees creaked in the rising wind. There were other noises; cries, far off, long, strange

67

howlings, the distant, unmistakable beat of a drum. And always the wind, gusting.

Late in the night they heard something else; a scream, suddenly cut off.

'That was a man,' Hakon whispered.

Brochael nodded, grimly.

'Shouldn't we go and see?'

'We're going nowhere, lad. Not until it's light.'

They tried to sleep, but the damp and the eerie nightsounds made it difficult. When Hakon finally woke Jessa to take her turn at the watch she felt as if she had drifted from one nightmare to another. She sat up, stiff and dirty.

'For Odinssake keep your eyes open,' Hakon muttered. 'This place terrifies me. I see what the old man meant.'

Irritably, she nodded, tugging out the long sharp knives from her belt. 'I know. Go to sleep, worrier.'

The fire was low; the mist smothering it. She fed it carefully, squatting with her back to the others. The horses tugged restlessly at their ropes; their ears flickering as a murmur of sound came from the wood. Jessa crouched, listening. She wondered where Kari's birds were. There was no sign of them, but they might be roosting up above, invisible in the black branches.

It took about half an hour for the kindling to run out.

Finally she stood up, brushing dead leaves from her knees. Gripping the knives tight, she ventured out cautiously into the trees, and looked around.

The wood was a dim gloom, mist drifting round the dark trunks. She crouched quickly, snatching up anything that would burn – pinecones, snapped twigs, branches. Suddenly her fingers touched something hard, and she lifted it, curious.

It was an old war-helmet, rusting away. One of the cheek-plates was gone; the empty eye-holes were clotted with soil. As she raised it the soil shifted and fell, as if the eyes had opened.

And something touched her.

She looked down, heart thudding.

A hand had been laid on her sleeve, softly. The fingers were scarred, pale as bone. And they had claws.

10

*Nine worlds I can reckon, nine roots of the
  tree,
The wonderful ash, way under the ground.*

Jessa screamed, twisting sideways. She jumped back,
crashing into Hakon; he caught her arm and dragged
her towards the fire, his eyes wide.

'Did you see it?' she gasped.

'There was a shadow . . . something.'

The wood around them was silent. For a long
moment they all stood listening, so tense that they
barely breathed, Jessa shuddering from cold and
shock.

Then Brochael hefted the axe in his hand. 'Get
some wood, Hakon. Plenty of it.'

They kept watch as Hakon sheathed his sword and
gathered quick armfuls of kindling, Jessa picking up
what he dropped. Then all of them backed to the
dying fire.

'Build it up,' Brochael ordered. He stood warily,
watching the dim trees. 'So what was it, Jessa?'

She took a deep breath. 'A hand. But the nails
were long, really long. For a moment I thought . . .'

'What?'

She shook her head. 'And there's this.'

70

She held up the helmet. He spared it a glance, then looked again, dubiously.

'That's familiar. Made at the Jarlshold, or Worms-head, surely.'

Skapti took it from her. 'Our people? Here?'

'Still here.' Kari was watching something, his frost-grey eyes moving, scanning the trees.

They looked at him and he said, 'You remember. Long ago an army from the Jarlshold marched north against the Snow-walkers. None of them ever came back, isn't that so? Except my father. And the witch was with him.'

Jessa nodded, remembering all too clearly. 'Mord told me that. He said the warband marched down into a strange white mist. No-one ever knew what happened to them. Presumably they died.' She looked into the fog, gathering round the trees. 'It happened here?'

'Near here.'

'But the hand I saw . . .'

'Dead men's nails grow,' Skapti said, drily.

She looked at him in horror. But Kari said, 'These are their ghosts. I can see them all around us. Gaunt, ragged men.'

'How many?' Brochael asked quietly.

'Too many.' Kari's voice was strained; he was glad they could not see as he could. The ghost army stood in the mist; wounded, filthy, their faces hard and unremembering, as if nothing of their lives or memory were left to them. They made no move, but their eyes were cold, and he knew they meant evil.

'Keep by the fire. I don't know what else we can do.'

Behind him the horses whinneyed; they too could

see. One reared, and then another, struggling frantically with their ropes. Turning, he saw the wraithmen had moved in behind, closer.

'Hold them!' Brochael snarled. 'If they break out we're in trouble.'

Hakon threw himself at the straining rope; he dragged the horses' heads down and Jessa grabbed the leading rein of the pack-horse, fighting to hang on to it. Slowly, they calmed the beasts, talking to them, rubbing their long noses, but they were still terrified, Jessa knew.

'What do we do?' Brochael said.

'Make a ring round the fire,' Kari answered. 'As close as you can. Lend me your sword, Hakon.'

For a moment Hakon hesitated. Then he held it out. Kari took it and held it a moment; then he put the point to the soil and drew a great circle around them, horses and all. Where the circle joined he stabbed the blade upright into the muddy ground; it swayed but stood.

Even before he had finished he saw the wraith-army run forward, heard their hissing snarls of disappointment.

Outside the circle they stood close, bleeding from old wounds, their eyes cold. He saw rusted swords in their hands, smashed shields, helms black with old blood.

'Don't go outside the ring,' Kari muttered. 'Whatever you do, don't break it.'

Jessa looked at his face, and the fear in it turned her cold. She stared outwards but saw nothing but trees, and mist, and faint movements in the corner of her eye, so that when she focussed on them they were gone. But she knew they were out there. The concentration of malice and fear was like a rank smell about them; she gave Hakon one of her long knives and he gave her a quick, grateful glance.

Then Kari spoke. 'I can hear you.'

He looked outward, at one spot. 'Leave us alone. These are your own people. Let them be.'

'We have no people,' the wraith-voice hissed at him. 'We have only the forest. We are its breath, its stirring. Our bodies feed its roots. We have waited years for you.'

'For me?' he breathed.

'A sorcerer as powerful as she was. Release us.'

There was silence. He knew the others were watching him; they had only heard his answers.

'What do they say?' Brochael growled.

Kari shook his head. Then he said, 'I'll do what I can. How will I find you?'

The ghost-warrior grinned, its broken face dark. 'We will show you the way, rune-lord.'

'When the sun comes.'

'Now.'

'No. When the sun comes.'

Silence answered him. He clenched his fists, alert for what they might do. But slowly, they moved back, and faded, into mist, into nothing. He let his breath out, painfully, and turned.

'They've gone.'

'Gone? Where? Will they be back?'

Kari pushed his hair from his eyes and sat down. 'They'll be back.'

All the rest of the night they sat alert around the fire, nervous of every sound. Kari seemed weary and preoccupied; he would say little about the ghost-army or what they had said to him, and soon drifted into sleep, his head on Brochael's chest.

'He can sleep anywhere,' Skapti muttered.

'He's lucky,' Hakon said.

None of the others could. They talked in low voices, uneasy, Skapti making bitter, defiant jokes about dead men. Slowly the wood lightened about them, the dawn-glint filtering through the massed leaves, but the mist still lingered, in pockets and hollows under the dark trees. Hakon's sword gleamed wet with dew.

Stiff, sore and thirsty, Jessa untwisted her hair and tied it up again, tight. Somehow that made her feel better. Skapti handed out bannocks and some of the dry, crumbly cheese, and they shared the cold water.

'There must be a stream nearby,' Jessa said.

'Probably.' The skald ate quickly, his eyes on the mist. 'But I'm not sure if I would care to drink from it.'

'Why not?' Hakon looked at him in alarm. 'What might it do?'

Skapti gave him a sharp sideways glance. 'There are streams in Ironwood that turn men to ice; make them sleep forever; drive them mad . . .'

'Skapti!' Brochael growled.

Hakon looked away, his face hot. 'I didn't believe any of it, anyway.'

When Kari woke, Brochael made him eat. 'Are they back yet, ravenmaster?' Skapti asked.

Kari nodded, swallowing. 'We have to follow them.'

'Follow them? Where?' Brochael demanded.

'I don't know. They've asked me to release them. Some sort of spell holds them here.'

74

'And if you can't?'

'Then we'll never leave the wood, Brochael. None of us.'

Jessa rubbed her chilled wrists. She caught Skapti's eye and he shrugged. 'That's one tale you can believe, Hakon.'

They mounted up, and Hakon heaved his sword out of the ground. At once Jessa felt unprotected, watched. They rode down the path that Skapti had found the night before. Around them the wood rustled, creaking with movement. All through the morning the realization grew in them that a crowd of invisible presences surrounded them; behind the creak of saddle-leather they began to hear the swish of feet through bracken and crisp drifts of leaves.

Soon Jessa grew wary of looking back; she had begun to see movements in the trees, to glimpse tall shapes that kept pace with them, and noticing Hakon's white, fixed look she guessed he had seen them too. None of them spoke now; Kari rode ahead, the ravens flapping over him; Brochael saying nothing, but watching, anxiously.

At midmorning they came to a hollow and rode down it in single file, the hooves crumbling the rich loam. At the bottom Kari paused, looking into the trees at the left of the path.

'In there.'

The plantation was dark, thickly overgrown. A curious smell came from it, musty; a smell of old, rotting things. Gently he eased his horse off the path, ducking under low branches. As the others followed, Brochael muttered, 'Weapons ready. All of you.'

Behind them, all around them, the wood seethed with its silent army, crowding between the trees.

75

Down Kari rode, almost lost ahead among the leaves, and then Jessa saw sunlight flicker on his hair, and she rode out after him into a great swathe of open land, choked with brambles and bracken.

They all stopped, looking ahead.

Before them was the mouth of a cave, huge, like the entrance to the underworld.

Jessa knew this was the place. It stank of death; flies buzzed in its windless silence. Among the bracken were heaps of rusted weapons, helms and shields, rotting into the soft soil. As the riders moved forward they felt as if the horses were treading among bones and snagged cloth and moss, sinking in deep. Disgusted, Jessa looked back. Among the trees she could see them now, the wraith-army, long-haired and gaunt, their faces cold and remote.

At the cave-mouth the travellers dismounted. Brochael peered into the dark. 'In there?'

'Yes.' Kari slipped past him, and the others followed, leaving the horses outside.

The cave was damp, dripping with water. Ferns sprouted from rock-crevices, and other blanched, unhealthy growths dripped liquid from their cold fronds. The shuffle of footsteps rang in the roof.

'How far in?' Hakon wondered.

'I don't know!' Jessa grinned at him. 'Worried?'

He pulled a face. 'All this witchery terrifies me. You know that.'

She nodded, thinking that not many people would have said it. But Hakon never pretended.

He slipped and she grabbed his elbow. 'Don't collapse on me.'

'It's getting darker.'

It was. As they left the entrance behind, the dim-

76

ness in front of them seemed thicker. Jessa stared into it, her nerves tight. Something was there, something dark, appalling.

Kari made some light. He lifted his hand and a glowing ring grew in the air, crackling with blue flames.

Hakon caught her arm. In the rune-light they saw a tree. A huge, dead ash tree. It was enormous; it towered above them into the roof of the cave, and far up in its bleached bare branches hung helmets and shields and the skulls of horses, turning and creaking slowly in the stillness. At the base of the tree a ring of swords had been rammed into the ground, between the spread roots.

As Kari stepped towards it she began to feel afraid of it; its branches were twisted and strangely askew, as if it had had more than tree-life, as if it had moved. Pulling out of Hakon's grip she jumped from rock to rock and landed just behind Kari.

'Wait!'

He turned.

'Don't go any nearer! I don't trust it.'

Behind her, Skapti said, 'She's right. This is an evil place. Only the gods know what went on here. And Gudrun.'

'You recognize it, then.'

They all did. The white snake was carved on the tree, into the heartwood, its lithe body winding round and round the dead, smooth bark, and the moss would not grow on it, as if the oozings of its skin poisoned them.

Kari took one step closer.

The crack rang in the roof; he and Jessa flung themselves aside, the branch crashing beside them,

77

scattering sand and bark. Raising her head she knew she was covered in dust; pain throbbed in her side where she'd bruised it against a rock.

Hakon hauled her up, roughly.

'Be careful!' she hissed.

Kari stood up too, the echoes of the fall dying in the roof.

They looked at the huge branch, split with age, tinder-dry.

Brochael turned to Kari. 'What do you want to do?'

'Burn it.' His voice was bleak and cold and he looked at them unhappily. 'This is the source of the spell. Burn it and they'll all be free.'

Brochael unsheathed his knife. 'At least there's plenty of kindling . . .' He stopped as Kari laid a hand on his arm. Glancing at the boy's face he said. 'I should have known it wouldn't be that easy.'

'Nothing will burn it except rune-fire.' He glanced back. 'Take the horses further away.'

Hakon went back, and caught the bridles, dragging the horses to a safer distance.

Kari stood near the tree, tiny in its shadow. High in the branches his two ravens perched and hopped among the twisting shields. At his call they swooped down to him.

He stood still. A draught of air ruffled his hair and the collar of his dark coat. Then, suddenly, he stepped back.

The tree shivered, as if a wind had passed through it. Then Jessa saw a flicker of red spark in the snake's belly; she saw it grow, crackling along the dry bark. Smoke formed a haze; the almost invisible flame roared along the lowest branches, and suddenly the tree was ablaze; an inferno of hot, blackening wood, spitting sparks high into the cave roof. And the snake, writhing among it, came twisting and slithering down, unwinding itself as if it would escape, blackening and opening into a roaring hole of heat. She caught hold of Kari and drew him away; then they both turned and ran for the cave mouth, stumbling among drifts of smoke and the stench of burning. Coughing, her face smarting and her eyes sore, Jessa looked into the forest.

The wraith-army waited.

'It's over,' Kari said to them.

For a moment, they stood there, watching the smoke stream from the cave. Then the ghost with the broken face nodded. 'Our thanks, sorceror. And a word of advice. The rainbow is not safe to walk on. Not for you.'

Kari glanced at the others. He knew they had not heard.

'And this warning is only for me?'

'Only for you.'

The wraith-army turned. Silently, they walked away.

11

*Boards shall be found of a beauty to wonder
   at,
Boards of gold in the grass long after,
The chess-boards they owned in olden days.*

All afternoon as they rode on, a mighty column of black smoke rose behind them, dissipating over the wood. Hours later, from higher ground, they looked back and could still see it, drifting east, the trees around them flexing and hissing in the rising gale.

'Why did she do it?' Jessa said thoughtfully.

'Spite.' Brochael was watching the sky. 'The same as with Signi. I don't like the look of this wind. We'll have rain. Maybe snow.'

Down among the dim aisles of trees they found a spring, bubbling cold and clear, and despite his wild tales Skapti was the first to drink from it. He sprawled against a fallen trunk and wiped his lips. 'Heart-ale. Sweeter than the mead of wisdom.' He looked round, considering. 'Why not stay here? It'll be dark soon.'

'No shelter.' Brochael filled his water-skin absently. 'We should find somewhere out of the rain.'

Jessa and Hakon exchanged grimaces. They were both tired out – only Kari had slept much the night before, and since the tree had burned he was silent and withdrawn, more so than usual.

Brochael must have noticed, because he said, 'We need a place where these youngsters can have a good rest. And the horses.'

'While we,' Skapti muttered, stretching out his long legs, 'we warriors, we Thor-like men of iron, travel tirelessly, I suppose?'

Brochael chuckled into his beard. 'Spindly poets don't need sleep. They dream enough in the daytime.'

For a while they sat there by the stream, eating the last strips of smoked venison that Ulf had given them, listening to the roar of the wind in the high branches. Since the spell-tree had burned, crashing in on itself into soft, powdery ash, the wood had changed. All that rustle and movement, the restless anger of the wraith-army, had gone. Under the roaring of the storm the wood was quiet. Its ghosts were sleeping.

They mounted up and rode on, now into squalls that gusted leaves and dust into their eyes. Jessa tied a scarf over her face and pulled her hood up, but soon the rain came, splattering between the trees. In minutes it was a heavy downpour, soaking them all, driving into their faces as they urged the wet horses on.

'This is useless!' Skapti shouted, as the wind caught his cloak and flung it against him. 'We need shelter!'

'Where?' Brochael roared back.

One of the ravens gusted down, landing with difficulty on a swaying branch. Kari watched it. Then he said, 'Not far ahead, it seems. There's a building.'

'A building? Here?'

'Some troll-nest,' Hakon muttered.

81

'I don't much care if it is; we'll look at it.' Brochael wiped sleet from his eyes. He looked up at the raven. 'Lead the way!'

At once it flew, low under the spread boughs and splintered oak-boles of this part of the forest, gliding like a shadow. They followed with difficulty through stunted hazels, and finally had to dismount and force their way through, dragging the reluctant horses.

Once off the path the undergrowth rose above them; a tangle of thorns and spiny bushes, menacing and almost impenetrable, as if they hid some secret place, lost for generations. Jessa was caught and snagged and tangled; she had to tear herself free more than once, and was ready to swear with frustration when she looked up, and saw the wall.

It loomed high over the trees, a black, strangely gabled shadow against the stormy sky. Clouds streamed above it; ivy or some other creeping growth covered it. There was no light, no sound of life.

Behind her, Hakon muttered. 'I was right. No man built that.'

The size of it silenced them; made them afraid. Sleet hissed into the trees around, tiny crystals of ice bouncing and scattering from leaf to leaf. The wind raged in their ears.

'What do you think?' Brochael said to Kari.

He shrugged. 'It looks old . . .'

Then he stopped. From far off in the forest had come a sound they all dreaded; that they had been waiting for for days, almost without knowing.

The rising howl of a wolf.

Others answered it, away to the east.

'That settles it.' Brochael shoved his way forward. 'Let's find the way in.'

They forced their way through the tangled growth and came to the base of the great wall. It rose above them; huge black blocks of hewn stone, so high it almost seemed to topple outwards. Saplings sprouted from it; ivy smothered it.

They groped their way along, searching for an entrance.

'It's ancient,' Jessa said.

Skapti nodded in the dimness. 'If this isn't a real giant-hall I don't know what is. What a size they must have been.'

Brochael, in front, laughed grimly. 'The bigger they are, the harder they fall.'

Ahead the wall reached a corner; he put his head round cautiously. Then he beckoned them on.

This seemed to be the front of the building. They passed two huge embrasures; deep in shadow and choked with tree-growth. Far above their heads they could dimly make out windows, immense and dark. Then they came to a small wall, knee-high. It took Jessa a moment to realize it was really a step.

She raised her head and looked up at the doorway in dismay. A mighty wooden door confronted them, the handle higher than Skapti's head. Two sprawling metal hinges interlaced across it, the bronze rivets green with age.

On each side were stone doorposts, three of them, the first carved into hundreds of faces, some dwarvish, others scowling, grinning, hostile or ugly; a tangle of leering looks sneering down at the travellers, their huge noses and beards and lips crumbling into wet stone. All across the lintel too the faces crowded, and among them here were skulls, and on the second doorpost strange inhuman things; trolls and wolves

and ettins and were-men, hideously open-mouthed.
Dragons finished the design, writhing about the third
row of posts, worm-like, biting each others' tails and
slavering over tiny men carved into crevices.

Us, Jessa thought.

Over everything else a great giant's face glared
down at those foolish enough to knock; it wore a
copper helm with nose and cheek guards; the face
was stern, with a thick stone beard and deepset eyes
that stared grimly from the shadows. Below it, in the
same odd script as before, were five runes; perhaps
his name.

GALAR

Rain splattered the carvings. The building was
silent and black.

'Well?' Skapti murmured uncomfortably.

'We'll open it. Hakon, come up here with me.'

Sword out, Hakon pushed through the horses to
Brochael. He rubbed his nose nervously, then gripped the sword-hilt tight with both hands.

They climbed the steep steps to the door.

Brochael reached up, straining, and grasped the
ring-handle. He turned it with all his strength, and
then pushed at the door. It stuck, the wood warped
and swollen. Skapti climbed up and helped them;
together they shoved hard, forcing a crack wide
enough for a horse to squeeze in. Then Brochael
said, 'Wait here.'

Axe in hand he slithered through the dark gap.

They waited, alert, in the cold rain. In about five
minutes he was back. 'Seems empty. Come on.'

They led the horses in one by one, the beasts
clattering nervously up the steps, their ears flicking
at unnameable sounds, baulking at the damp black

entrance. Jessa had to walk hers in backwards, coaxing and cursing him under her breath. Once inside, she gripped the harness and stared around.

They stood in a huge darkness. Nothing could be seen of the hall but a glimmer of dusky sky here and there, far up in the roof, as if in places the turf or wood had worn and crumbled to holes.

'No windows.' Hakon's voice came suddenly out of the dark.

'Must be. We saw them.' They heard Brochael fumbling for his fire-box.

'Smothered by ivy,' Jessa suggested.

'Or shutters.'

They heard Brochael mutter to Kari, and a small blue flame suddenly cracked into the darkness. It steadied into yellow, burning on the end of a thin beeswax taper. Brochael was grinning, as if at some joke.

'Now,' he said, gripping the axe. 'Let's see where we are.'

'What about the door?' Skapti said.

'Ah yes. Close it.'

But although they all pushed together it was wedged now, immovable.

'Oh leave it,' Jessa gasped at last. 'At least we can get out.'

'And anything else can get in!'

'The birds will stay outside,' Kari said. 'They'll warn us.'

'Right,' Brochael said. 'Follow me.'

Carefully, they moved out over the smooth dark floor. Judging from the muffled thump of the hooves it wasn't stone but trampled earth, Jessa thought. The flame above Brochael's hand was tiny; it flung

85

a huge distorted shadow of him back across their faces. The others were barely visible; glimpses of eyes and faces. As they crossed it she knew the hall was even more huge than it had seemed from outside. Here and there weeds and fat pale mushrooms sprouted, glistening wet in the candleflame. All around hung heavy silence, and far behind the pale crack of the doorway glimmered.

'Over here,' Brochael whispered. He shaded the flame with his hand and turned to the left, walking more quickly. He came to something dark and bent over it; then he picked it up.

'Look at this.'

It was a carved horse, a chess-piece. It was as long as his arm.

They gathered round it, fingering the rotting wooden mane. Other chess-pieces lay on the floor, scattered around, broken and softening into the soil. Kari knelt and touched one, lingering over it.

'Long dead,' Brochael said stoutly, but there was a question behind it. Kari took his hand off the king-piece and looked around in the darkness. 'A wolf is listening,' he said.

Far off, as if to answer him, one howled in the wood.

'They won't come in here,' Jessa said.

He looked at her strangely, but said nothing.

Walking between the huge chess-pieces they crossed to the end of the hall. Here a doorway led off into another room, pitch black. Weapons in hand, they went in.

This room was smaller; a pale window at one end showed them a patch of stormy sky and two stars, glinting. Wind roared through it. Debris was scattered here too, and in one corner a tree-trunk had sprouted up and died and fallen, years ago; now it lay in a sprawling tangle.

Brochael slapped it. 'This will do. Plenty of kindling. We can watch the doorway to the hall.'

'There's another door down there,' Skapti muttered, straining his eyes into the gloom. 'This place is a warren.'

Brochael stuck the candle into a crack in the tree-trunk and began to gather scraps of wood. They snapped easily, dry and loud.

It took no time to get a fire going; the flames lit the corner of the great room but little else. The travellers dried themselves out and ate wearily, then wriggled into blankets almost without a word. Jessa was glad to be warm. As she tossed to find a comfortable position she thought of the old man, back at Ulf's. He had said something about a great hall. The thought eluded her; she was too tired to chase it. Sleep swallowed her instantly, like a great wolf.

Hakon had first watch.

He propped his chin on his sword to keep awake, but that was no use; soon he was nodding, and had to get up and prowl about in the dark.

He crossed to the doorway and gazed out, into the black spaces. For a moment he had thought that something had shuffled out there, but everything seemed still. Far across, he could see the crack of the outer doorway, paler than the surrounding blackness.

The others were asleep; it would be better not to wake them unless he was sure. If it was nothing, Skapti would have something bitterly sarcastic to say. Jessa too, if he knew her.

He stared out, puzzled, into the hall. The silence

of the great ruin was complete. He thought of the warped doors, the dust over everything. No-one could be still here.

Then, this time nearer, he heard it again. A chink of sound.

Gripping his sword-hilt with both hands, Hakon stepped cautiously out, sliding his foot against rubble and stones. Out in the invisible heart of the hall a patch of moonlight fell briefly through a roof-hole and vanished; he glimpsed sleet spiralling down and for a moment something long and grey that moved through it and slid into the dark. His heart thumped. It had looked like a wolf.

He waited, breathless a moment, then took a silent step back. At once a cold hand slid around his mouth and clamped down; a swordpoint jabbed in his back.

'Don't move. Make a sound and I cut your throat.'

The swordpoint was a cold pain between his shoulderblades; even breathing out made him wince with the sharp stab. The hand lifted from his mouth and took his sword, quickly. Rigid, Hakon squirmed with fury. He wanted desperately to call out, but dared not. And yet the others were depending on him. He opened his mouth but it was too late; the hand clamped back.

'How many of you are there?' the hoarse voice whispered.

Hakon shook his head.

'How many?' The hand lifted, slightly.

He managed a yell, half-stifled, but loud; then he was turned and shoved face-first into the wall, a bruising blow that burst in his forehead, and to his astonishment and fear the room growled about him, it rumbled and shook, and the floor tilted and he fell, into a slither of stones.

12

A wind-age, a wolf-age, till the world ruins;
No man to another shall mercy show.

Jessa woke to a roaring and rumble that made the floor shake. Pain sprang in her fingers; for a moment she thought they had been bitten off; memory and sleep confused her. Far off in the building something slid and smashed. One of the horses was whinnying with terror; as she watched, Brochael's pack slipped from the tree-trunk and crashed down, spilling water and food and coins that rolled and rattled.

Skapti hauled her up.

'What is it?' she gasped.

'Keep quiet!'

Silent, they waited, letting the long echoes fade. The walls quivered once, and were still.

'An earthquake?' Skapti breathed.

Something crashed out in the hall, settling to stillness.

'Could be.' Brochael stood tense. 'If so we should get outside. There'll be others.'

'It could have been something else,' Jessa muttered.

'A giant, walking?' Skapti suggested.

They were silent, despite the scorn in his tone,

90

imagining the great figure of Galar pacing through his hall. Then behind them, in the firelight, Kari said, 'Brochael. Hakon's missing.'

They all turned, instinctively. 'The fool!' Brochael hissed. 'What was he thinking of? Has he gone outside?'

'No. The birds would say.' Kari looked preoccupied. Abruptly he said, 'I think there's someone else here – out there in the hall.'

They gazed apprehensively at the black archway. Then Brochael walked up to it, and even his great bulk was tiny in its shadows.

'Hakon?' he breathed.

A small, strangled murmur came out of the darkness. Then Hakon's voice, sounding strained. 'I'm all right Brochael, but there's someone with me.'

'Who?'

Only silence answered.

'Get me some light,' Brochael snapped.

Carefully, Skapti went and pulled a smouldering branch from the fire; he lit the candle with it. Light glimmered on the wild eyes of the horses as they backed and snorted.

'Leave the boy alone,' said Brochael hotly. 'If he's hurt . . .'

'Listen!' Hakon sounded breathless. 'He's got a sword at my throat. He says he's alone and wants no trouble, but if you attack he'll kill me.'

'We should all get outside,' Skapti muttered. 'That earthquake . . .'

'I know! But Hakon first. Come on.'

They stepped out behind him, through the arch.

The candlelight was weak; eventually it showed them Hakon, crouched among a pile of stones with his knees up under him and his head dragged back; a blade glimmered under his chin. In the faint light someone else stood behind him, grey and shapeless. Dust was spiralling everywhere, and what looked like snow drifted through the roof-gaps.

'Let him go!' Brochael hissed.

Hakon was dragged, clumsily, upright. The shadowy figure was tall and lean. But no giant.

'If I do,' a low voice said, 'then we meet as friends?'

'For our part.' Skapti was dangerously quiet.

They waited. Then Hakon stumbled forward and stepped away, quickly, as if he had been released, and they heard the long shiver of steel returning to its sheath.

The man gave Hakon his sword back and lifted his hands. 'No weapons.'

Reluctantly, Skapti put his sword away and Jessa her knife. Brochael let the axe swing from its strap around his wrist. Kari did not move.

'Come to the fire,' Brochael said gruffly. Turning, he muttered, 'And let's have a look at you.'

The man came behind them, gradually, into the light. He was tall and hooded, and as he pushed the hood back they saw that his hair was grey and long, swept back to the nape of his neck. He had bright, amber-coloured eyes and a fine grey stubble of beard. He would be about forty, Jessa thought, quite old; a strong, lean man, in colourless clothes. He wore no amulets, no brooches, no metal of any kind except his sword, in its battered leather scabbard.

'Are you really alone?' Skapti asked.

'I am now.' The man spoke huskily; his front teeth were sharply pointed, as if they had been filed.

Brochael glanced at Kari, who nodded, almost imperceptibly. The stranger gazed warily around at them. His glance caught on Kari, just for an instant, and a flicker passed over his face but he said nothing. Jessa had noticed it though; she knew Kari would have too.

'I'm a traveller through this wood, as you are,' the stranger said, taking the food that Skapti held out to him. 'I came from the west; I've been searching many weeks for the giants' road. When I found it I followed it. It led me here.' He looked round, wryly. 'I watched you come. I needed to be sure you were indeed men.'

'What were you afraid we might be?' Kari asked, unexpectedly.

The grey man gave him a shrewd glance. 'Anything, lord. Trolls, were-beasts. Even Snow-walkers.'

There was a tense silence. Jessa fingered her knife-hilt.

Kari nodded. 'You know I am one of that people.'

'I see that.'

'You've known others?'

'I've had dealings with them.' The man's voice was almost a growl. He said no more; no-one pressed him.

Instead Skapti said, 'We're travelling to the country of the Snow-walkers. Do you know where that is?'

'Over the edge of the world. No-one can get there.' But even as he said it Jessa saw the considering look in his eyes.

'You haven't told us your name,' she said.

He looked away. 'I have no name. Not now. I'm an outlaw, without kin.'

'But we have to call you something.'

He looked at her strangely. 'Do you? Then I choose a name. A name out of this wood. I choose Moongarm.'

They stared at him in silence. Jessa remembered Skapti's story of the wolf that would devour the moon. Moongarm. And to be an outlaw meant the man was a murderer at least, or under some curse.

'You choose a grim name,' Brochael said heavily.

'I have a grim humour.'

He held out his hands to the fire; the backs of them were covered with fine grey hairs, the nails blackened and broken. 'Will you allow me to travel with you? The forest is no place for a man alone.'

Instantly, they all felt uneasy. 'We need to speak about that,' Brochael said, stonily.

'Then do.' Moongarm stood up. 'I'll fetch my goods, out there in the hall.' He walked out, with long strides.

Brochael turned. 'I say no. An outcast – probably a murderer. He has that look. We'd never be able to trust him.'

'Not only that,' Skapti said, 'he's cheerless as the grave.'

'Be serious!'

'Oh I am! But if you don't trust him, Brochael, we should have him with us. Or do you want him out there in the forest following us, as he will; not knowing at every night's camp which tree he's looking down from?'

Jessa nodded. 'Skapti's right. We need to keep an eye on him. And there are five of us.'

'Hakon?'

Hakon scowled. 'I don't want him. If I'd been on my own he'd have killed me.'

Somehow they all felt that was true.

Brochael shrugged and looked at Kari. 'It's up to you.'

For a moment Kari said nothing. Then, quietly, 'I think we should let him stay.'

'But why?'

Unhappily he looked beyond them, his eyes bright and frost-pale. 'I don't know yet. He has something to do with us. And like Skapti I would rather know where he is.' A change in his expression warned them and they saw the man come back through the arch, a heavy pack in his arms. He threw it down in a corner.

'Is it to be?'

Brochael rubbed his beard with the back of his hand and breathed out, exasperated. 'It seems so. But I'm warning you, Moongarm . . .'

'I hear you, tawny man.' He smiled then, showing his teeth. 'To show faith I'll even take the first watch.'

'You will not,' Brochael snarled. 'Besides, we're moving out. That earthquake . . .'

'. . . Was no earthquake.' Moongarm spread a moth-eaten blanket out in the corner, calmly. 'I know a little about this hall. Traveller's tales. They say the giant who lived in it still lives; that he was buried alive near here by the gods themselves, centuries ago. He struggles and squirms to be free, and his struggles shake the ground.'

They were silent a moment. Then Skapti said, 'A good tale.'

'It's true. Tomorrow, I'll show you the place.'

'Where?' Jessa asked.

'A little north of here.'

She nodded. 'And if you came from the west how do you know about it? How long have you been living in this hall?'

Sharply, he turned and looked at her. Then he smiled, and shook his head, rolled himself in the blanket and turned his back on them.

As they settled down Jessa moved nearer to Kari. 'Is he safe?'

'For the moment.' He lay on his back, staring up at the black spaces of the roof. 'There's a lot he hasn't told us. Did you notice his ears?'

She shook her head.

'Look at them tomorrow.'

'But he's got no horse. He'll slow us down. And we need to hurry, Kari. Anything could be happening back at the hold.' She wriggled into the woven blanket, trying to get warm. 'I wonder how Wulfgar is managing.'

'So do I,' Kari said, softly.

Later, when he was sure they were all sound asleep he unfolded from his body and left them, stepping soundlessly past Brochael at the door. It cost him too much strength to do this often, but tonight he was restless. Moongarm worried him. There were scents and tastes and tingles about the man which were alien; he smelt of sorcery and rank, animal things.

Kari could have reached into the man's mind, but he held back, as he always did. That was how Gudrun had started, controlling the men around her. He feared that for himself. And so far, the stranger had done nothing except lie. And yes, that flicker of recognition. Kari had felt that, like a feather across his

96

face. And more, a flash of old hatred, instantly snapped off.

Now he walked, silent as a ghost across the empty hall, through an enormous doorway to the base of a stair, each step high as his waist. Quickly he hauled himself up, his spirit-body light and frail as a cobweb, and as he climbed the air grew colder; the steps froze under his fingers.

At the top was a great platform, covered with a thin crust of snow, the parapet cracked and broken. He crossed to the edge and looked out over the forest, high above the trees.

Closing his eyes he moved into the distance, with a great effort. He saw the Jarlshold, the dark houses, the watchman coughing outside the hall door.

Things were worse.

He knew that at once. Signi still slept, and of her soul there was no sign. But others were here now, wandering the purple twilight, trapped in the power of his spell-ring. Two old men, a woman, a warrior – he knew all their faces, one or two of their names. They had been well enough when he left. The little boy was with them. He watched them walk restlessly between the houses, and the wind of dreams that blew there was stronger; it rattled doors and gusted against the walls of the hall.

He dragged his mind back to the giant-hall and opened his eyes.

Jessa was right, as usual.

They would need to hurry.

13

The brood of Fenris are bred there,
Wolf-monsters.

'Near here,' Moongarm said abruptly, 'is the burial place I told you about.'

They looked down at him, curiously. It was the first time he had spoken since they'd left the giant-hall, after another, milder ground-shake had woken them all. Since then the grey man had walked tirelessly beside the horses. Brochael had grudgingly offered him the pack-pony but he had refused, saying the beast disliked him. Jessa had noticed that all the horses did, whickering and rolling their eyes whenever he came too close.

Now, remembering what Kari had said, she looked at his ears. They seemed oddly placed, hidden by his hair. She glanced at Kari but he was gazing into the wood, lost in his thoughts.

The morning was bitterly cold; a thin layer of snow lay where the trees were sparse. It struck her how the weather was changing quickly – too quickly – as they travelled north. At the Jarlshold it had been midsummer. Now they already seemed to be riding into winter, as if they travelled in time, as well as distance.

They came to a wide place which had been cleared of trees long ago. Saplings had sprouted up but the frequent earthquakes had toppled and uprooted them; the whole area was a mass of tumbled rock and earth piled high, without shape, as if it had been shattered and heaved up, over and over.

'This is it,' Moongarm said.

Brochael gazed around. 'It seems like an ordinary landslip,' he said, coldly.

'And that.' The grey man pointed. 'What does that seem like?'

To their left, in a patch of sandy soil, something stuck out from the earth. It was big, a hard, shiny thing, curved like a shield, split and broken, blackened with dirt and age. As she stared at it Jessa saw it move, just a fraction.

At once soil slid; stones rattled. The ground began to rumble, a far-off deep tremble. The forest floor quivered, a tree crashing behind them.

'Out!' Brochael yelled, wheeling round; then they were all galloping for the trees, Moongarm racing after them.

The ground bubbled; it heaved and bucked as if something huge was indeed raging and struggling underneath, and only when they were well into the trees did it stop, and they felt safe.

'Did you see that?' Jessa gasped, fighting to control her horse.

'I did indeed.' Skapti looked at her slyly. 'What did it look like, Jessa?'

She flicked her hair from her eyes, reluctant. 'You know what.'

'Tell me.'

She glared at him, annoyed. 'All right, if you're all

99

too scared to put words on it. It looked like a thumb-nail. A huge thumbnail sticking up out of the ground. As if the rest of the hand was buried down there. Not even poets could make that up.'

Skapti grinned. 'What a poem this will be.'

'The poem can keep.' Brochael turned his horse and glared darkly down at Moongarm. 'This is no place for us.'

All that day, and all the next, they rode north through the endless wood, keeping to what remained of the road, and the air became crisp with frost. Already they wore thicker clothes; the packhorse travelled light, all the food almost gone. On the second evening Hakon caught a hare in a snare; they stewed it with mushrooms and puffball, and the juices were hot and sweet, a welcome change from dry meat and salt fish. But there was barely enough.

Even the length of the days had begun to shorten; winter was closing about them, the eternal cold of the north. Snow drifted often between the trees; the nights were bitter, uncomfortable times, spent as close to the fires as was safe.

Moongarm travelled tirelessly, easily keeping up in the tangled undergrowth that slowed them. On more open stretches, where the horses could briefly run, he loped behind, the ravens above him. Jessa was sure they were watching him. Brochael's glance too, often followed him suspiciously; Moongarm was well aware of this, and seemed not to care. In fact she thought Brochael stayed awake through Moongarm's watches, despite the ravens on the branch overhead. But the stranger did nothing. He walked silently, and ate his food to one side.

On the third afternoon after the giant-hall the

100

wood became such a tangled murk that they had to dismount and hack their way through, dragging the reluctant horses. The road, all that was left of it, was completely lost under leaf-litter; the black gloom of the crowding, silent wood made them all uneasy. They felt they were deep in the forest, lost in it, that they would never come out. Far behind a wolf howled, then another, nearer.

'That's all we need.' Hakon stumbled over a tree-root and rubbed dirt wearily from his face. 'Gods, I'm filthy. What I wouldn't give for a bed. And hot food. And wine!'

'Wine!' Jessa said, scornfully. 'A few months ago you'd never even tasted it!'

'It doesn't take long to get that hankering,' Skapti muttered. 'Wine. Odin's holy drink.' He slashed a branch aside with his sword. 'What do you say, grey man?'

Moongarm looked at him briefly. 'Water is my drink.'

'Water's good enough,' Skapti observed. 'For washing.'

Moongarm smiled narrowly. 'As you say.' He looked into the trees on his right. 'But I hear a stream nearby, and I'm thirsty.'

He shoved his body into the mass of leaves and almost disappeared; after a moment Kari led his horse in after him.

'We'll catch you up,' he said.

The others struggled on, deeper into the wood. 'Aren't you going to stay and watch him?' Jessa teased.

Brochael frowned at her. 'Kari can look after himself. And besides . . .'

A twig cracked, sharp, to his left.

He spun around.

A flurry of men in green, a sudden, bewildering ambush, were leaping and falling from trees and rocks, swift as thought. Hakon crashed down; Skapti yelled a warning. Already Brochael was struggling with two of them; another grabbed Jessa from behind. She screamed; the horse reared and as the man glanced up at it she saw his face, hungry, mud-smeared, leering. She drew her knife and struck without a thought, slashing his arm, the blood welling instantly.

Brochael was up, swinging his axe; there was a wary space around him. As she turned she saw something flicker at his back; her eyes widened with fear.

'Behind you!'

But the arrow, swifter than words, was in him. He slammed back against a tree, crumpled up, and lay still.

14

At the host Odin hurled his spear.

'Brochael!'

Kari's voice was a scream of anguish.

He ran from the trees; already the archer was fitting another arrow. Jessa yelled at him, wild, desperate. She saw Kari kneel, his face white and cold, and then he turned and struck – she almost saw it, that savage, flung bolt of power.

The archer crumpled with a scream. Face down in the mud he smacked, and the searing crackle of that death rang in the wood.

For one shocked instant the attackers were still; then they were gone, as if the trees had absorbed them.

It had been so quick. Jessa was dizzy with the speed of it.

Skapti picked himself up and hobbled to Brochael, turning him gently.

'Is he dead?'

'No, Jessa. Your shout warned him enough. It's the shoulder. But it'll have to come out.' Working quickly, Skapti staunched the blood.

She glanced at Kari. He was white, his hands knotted together.

Moongarm bent over the outlaw. He glanced up

at Kari with a strange fear on his face. 'Well, this one is.'

The Snow-walker looked over at Moongarm, at first as if he barely understood. Then he went and stared down at the man, and rubbed his hand over his forehead.

'I didn't mean this.'

'It looked final enough to me.'

Kari gave Moongarm a fierce look and went back to Brochael.

'Can't you keep quiet,' Hakon muttered.

Moongarm shrugged.

'Get the horses,' Skapti said over his shoulder. 'We can't stay here. They may come back.'

'I doubt it,' Moongarm said.

'So do I!' the skald yelled at him, suddenly furious. 'But I'm taking no chances! Get Brochael on my horse. Quickly!'

They rode warily, hurriedly, deeper into the tangled wood. Hakon was in front and Moongarm watched their backs, sword drawn. Jessa kept near Kari, who was silent. So was she. She hardly knew what to say.

When they found a defensible cleft in some rocks they eased Brochael down, Skapti and Hakon taking his weight. They lit a fire, and the skald worked on the wound, probing it with his fingers and a thin knife, muttering to himself.

Kari watched, bleakly, and when it was over and Brochael slept he went and sat against a tree-trunk. The ravens hunched unnoticed at his feet.

Jessa went and sat with him. 'He's strong. He'll be all right,' she said.

He nodded.

'You had to do it,' she went on, awkwardly.

'I killed him. I wanted him dead.'

'Easy to understand.'

He gave her a glance that chilled her. 'Yes. Many people feel that. But I can do it, just by a thought. I let myself do it.'

He was shaking with shock and misery. She put her arm around him and they sat there for a while, watching Skapti build up the fire.

'Hakon will be jealous,' Kari said at last.

Jessa stared in surprise. 'Will he?'

He almost smiled. Then he said, 'When Brochael went down like that, Jessa, I felt as if it was me, as if it had struck me, right through the heart.'

She nodded. She knew that already.

Later, when Kari was asleep, she said to Skapti, 'Who were they, do you think?'

He shrugged. 'Outlaws. Kinless men.'

She looked at Brochael, restless and flushed in the fire's heat. 'He will be all right?'

The skald ran a thumb down his stubbly chin. 'I'm no expert, Jessa. I'd say so, if we can keep the wound clean. He's a strong man. But we need a place to rest up, and I don't know if it's safe enough here.'

'I can make sure of that.' Moongarm squatted beside them in the dimness. 'I'll go and prowl around. Make sure we've not been followed.'

Skapti shook his lank hair. 'It's too dangerous. We can't afford to lose you too.'

'So you need me now?'

'We need everyone,' Skapti stared at him levelly, 'if we're all going to get out of here alive.'

'I'll be safe enough. No-one will see me.'

He turned away into the shadows; Skapti muttered, 'Fool'.

He started to get up, but Jessa put her hand on his. 'Let him go.'

He looked at her.

'Let him go. I think he knows what he's doing. I think he knows this wood better than we do.'

They stayed in the clearing by the rocks for a day and a night. Moongarm came back soon after daylight, saying he had searched the forest around the camp as far as he could; there were no signs of the outlaws. The body they had left behind still lay there.

'Let the wolves have it,' Hakon muttered.

Moongarm gave him a searching look. 'They already have.'

Brochael slept for a few hours, then ate the food Kari brought him. He was cheerful, and joked about the pain. Skapti had told him what had happened, but he said nothing until Karl did.

'Death comes to us all. That's fate.'

'Not his death. It wasn't a fair fight.'

Brochael snorted. 'You think it would have been, if you'd fought him with a sword?'

'It wouldn't have been fair to you then,' Jessa said.

Kari glared at her, irritably. 'Thank you for reminding me.'

'We each use our strengths,' Brochael said. 'A sword for some of us. Jessa has her brains, Skapti his lore.'

'And I have sorcery.'

'Many would envy you,' Brochael said quietly.

'Not if they knew.'

On the second day they left, travelling slowly. Brochael did not complain, though Jessa guessed the wound must be burning him. But he laughed at her sympathy.

'Don't worry about me, little valkyrie. I've had a hard life.'

By midday the trees had begun to thin: finally Skapti pushed through a thicket and stopped. His voice came back to them strangely unmuffled.

'Look at this!'

Jessa broke through the cover, quickly, and grinned as the cold clear air struck her face and lifted her hair; behind her Hakon gave a whoop of delight.

At last, the forest had ended. They were on a high fellside, and below them spread a new country of lakes and open slopes, white with untrodden snow. Mountains rose to the north and east, huge and astonishingly near, their tips scarlet with the smouldering sunset.

Brochael and Kari emerged behind them, leaves in their hair. Kari looked tired and Brochael gruff-tempered, but their faces cleared at the sight of the wide, bare country.

'Thank the gods for that,' Brochael roared. 'Another day of trees and I would have run mad!'

A flock of birds scattered at his shout.

'You're mad already,' Skapti said mildly. Then he whistled. 'Have you seen what you're standing under?'

He reached into a hollybush and pushed branches aside, carefully, and they saw that a great archway rose over them, almost completely masked by growth. The same strange runes ran around it, and on the top, glaring down at them between the red berries, was the stern, helmed face that had guarded the hall.

'Galar,' said Jessa. 'I wonder if he's the one who's buried.'

'If it is I'm glad he can't get up.' Hakon looked at Skapti. 'This must mark the end of his land.'

'The end of the wood. The wood is his.'

'So where now?'

Brochael grimaced. 'Down. Before night.'

But it was dark well before they reached the bottom of the steep, unstable slope, winding down on the broken path, between rocks and stunted trees to the silent land below. In the end Hakon's horse slipped suddenly and crashed heavily onto its knees; he fell clear, but the horse did not get up; it struggled bitterly but the foreleg was broken, everyone could see.

'It's finished,' Brochael said grimly. 'Get your pack off it, Hakon.'

When his gear was off Hakon loaded it onto the pack-beast; they led the other horses carefully down the rest of the ravine.

Brochael stayed behind.

When he came down into the camp they had made, some time later, the long knife he wore had been scrupulously cleaned. He carried a sack under his arm.

Stiff and sore, he sat down. 'No spare horses now.' Jessa gave him some smoked fish; he chewed it thoughtfully. 'At least we've got some fresh meat. Tomorrow, we'll cook it. You, Moongarm . . .'

He looked round, quickly. 'Where is he?'

108

The man's pack was there, but there was no sign of him.

'Now where's he lurking?' Brochael growled. 'I don't trust him. Not even when I can see him.'

'The birds are with him,' Kari said quietly. 'He won't be far.'

Later, deep in the night, Jessa rolled over and saw Moongarm come into camp and talk to Skapti, quietly. The grey man looked sleek somehow. He refused any food and lay down, on his own as usual.

Jessa caught Skapti's eye and lifted her eyebrows. The skald shrugged.

Not far off, she could hear wolves snarling and fighting over the carcase of the horse, where it lay under the stars.

15

Fairer than sunlight, I see a hall,
A hall thatched with gold.

The village was floating on the water.

That was Jessa's first thought, as she gazed down at it from the deep snow of the hillside. Then she realized it was built on an island, or on some ingenious structure of high poles out there in the misty lake. A narrow wooden causeway linked it to the bank, built high over the marshlands, leading to a gate, firmly shut. A tall pallisade guarded the village from attack. From one or two of the houses smoke drifted into the purple sky, up into the veils of aurora that flickered like ghost-light over the brilliant stars.

It looked safe, snug behind its defences.

And very quiet.

Brochael shifted, pulling the stiff, frosted scarf from his mouth. 'Well?' he said, gruffly.

They had been four days now living off horsemeat and herbage and melted snow. The horses limped with the cold; their riders ached with weariness and hunger. Each of them knew the settlement was a godsend.

Only Moongarm seemed uneasy.

'Are you coming with us?' Brochael glared at him sourly. 'You don't have to.'

The grey man turned his strange amber eyes on him. 'You know how much you'd miss me, Brochael. Don't worry, I'll come.'

'You would!' Brochael scowled.

As they picked their way down Jessa wriggled her toes with relief. She was starving, and stiff with cold. Hakon grinned at her. There was no doubt what he thought.

Snow fell silently about them, small hard flakes that rolled from hair and shoulders and melted slowly, soaking through cloth. It fell on the dark lake water and glittered, the northern lights catching the brief scatter of crystal. On the hillside it lay thick, banked in great drifts, and the horses' hooves drove deep holes into it, compacting it to ice with careful, crunching steps.

Long before they reached the marsh they were challenged. A question rang out; Brochael stopped them at once, very still.

'Travellers,' he roared, his voice ringing in the hard frost. 'Looking for a welcome.'

There was silence. An aurora whispered overhead.

Then two figures stepped out of the darkness, well-muffled, with flat snow-shoes strapped under their feet. One carried a long glinting spear; the other, whose eyes alone were visible in the wrappings about his face, had a peculiar weapon – a wand of wood, studded with quartz and crystals and tiny silver bells that tinkled in the cold.

They looked up warily at the travellers.

The man with the wand had bright, sharp eyes. He raised his hand.

111

'We give our hospitality to anyone, strangers, but especially at this time. Tomorrow is a great feast day for us, so you've come at a good time.'

He came forward and held up his hand to Brochael. Brochael leaned down and gripped it. 'Our thanks.'

The man nodded. 'You'll need to lead those beasts of yours. The causeway is slippery with ice. Follow me.'

They dismounted into the soft snow.

'Can't see much of them,' Hakon muttered.

'Well they can't see much of us,' Jessa winked at him. 'They might not like your face when they do. Keep your sword handy.'

The causeway began in the snow and stretched out over the bog; a narrow, railed walkway, built of split logs caulked and spread with what smelt like resin or pitch, a sharp smell. The horses thudded over, noisily. Below them the marsh spread; its stiff stalks and frozen rushes purple in the aurora-light, with strange wisps of blue that rose and drifted in the mist. Somewhere, waterfowl quacked. The marsh smelt dank, of decay, of a million rotting stems.

As they walked further out, black water glinted beneath them. Jessa saw how the snow lay in a thin film across it, already freezing in patches. Tomorrow the lake would be sealed under a frozen lid.

At the end of the causeway was the gate. The wand-man knocked and called; the heavy wooden door swung open. Inside, figures came running out from nearby houses; some to stare, others to help, pulling the horses into a low building lit with lanterns, its empty stalls spread with fresh rushes and shavings.

'Unload your goods,' the man said, 'and bring them with you, whatever you need. These men will see to your horses.'

He waited for them, after whispering something to a small figure who slipped out at once. A girl, Jessa thought. She slung the bag on her sore shoulders and moved up next to Kari.

'Are we safe here?' she asked quietly.

'He pushed his hood off and looked at her gravely. 'I don't know, Jessa! I don't know everything.'

'Sorry.' She grimaced. 'We'll find out soon enough, I suppose.'

'No-one attacks their guests.' Hakon sounded shocked.

Skapti shrugged, behind him. 'It's been known.'

'Only in sagas!'

'Sagas are real, I've told you that. As real as your sword, dream-wielder.'

The stranger led them out of the byre, across the trampled snow. A low, rectangular building was nearby; the door so sunken that the snow was already banked against it. The man stopped and opened it, trudging down a pathway. He beckoned them in.

The smoke caught Jessa's throat as she straightened, making her eyes smart; as she coughed the light of many candles flared and danced around her. Then they steadied. She saw a small, airless room, acrid with smoke. After the clear cold air outside it felt stiflingly warm. The hearth was in the centre; a great bronze cauldron hung over it on a triple chain. Above, the thatch was yellow, pale as gold.

Sitting round the cauldron, staring at her, was a small group of men and women, obviously one family. They were all heavily tattooed. Each of them

113

had some thin blue creature crawling down his or her cheek; a boar or a fox or a fish. A small, elderly man, the man who stood up, had a strange coiling beast of curling dots. Their hair was dark and glossy, their clothes brilliantly coloured; woven wool and dyed seal-skin in reds and greens and blues, all hung with knots and luckstones and feathers.

'Welcome,' the chieftain said warmly, his accent strange. 'Come to the fire, all of you.'

For a moment no-one moved. Then Brochael dumped his pack against the wall and came forward. The others followed, pulling off coats and wrappings and gloves, scattering snow on the floor and benches.

'Come close, come,' the old man insisted, waving them in. He said something quietly; a woman and a girl got up and poured out a drink for each of them, handing out small horns of yellow-coloured liquid.

Skapti tasted it and smiled in surprise. 'Mead?'

'We call it honey-brew. Sit down now, be comfortable.'

There were low benches near the hearth; the travellers perched themselves in a thankful row. The man who had brought them in pulled off his own faceguard and coat; now he came and sat near them, laying the quartz-headed wand carefully at his feet. The bells gave a strange, silvery chink. Not a weapon, Jessa thought suddenly. Something magical.

She looked at him curiously. He had a lean, sharp face, with a ragged fringe of brown hair. A tattoo uncoiled on his cheek, ran down his neck and under his clothes. Two others crawled on the backs of his hands. The silver bells showed that he was someone special; a shaman, she thought firmly, noticing the strange pierced bones that hung from his belt.

Food was set before them and they ate, hungrily. Hot roast spicy meats, possibly duck; fish, fresh from the lake; crumbly oatcakes and honey, cheese and beer. It was a feast, and Jessa enjoyed it to the full, despite the stifling smoke. It had been weeks since they'd eaten properly; she noticed how thin and gaunt they all looked, how travel-worn. Filthy, long-haired, wild.

The chieftain watched them. His eyes were light-blue, his face beginning to wrinkle. He smiled. 'My name is Torvi, father of the people. This is my wife Yrsa and my daughter Lenna. The Speaker is our wiseman, our shaman to the dark. His own name may not be known.'

As he said that the family made a brief sign, a touching of their lips. Jessa nodded to herself. Knowing his name would give them power over him. Or so these people would believe.

Skapti gave their own names courteously and the tattooed people gazed at them all. If they recognized what Kari was, they said nothing. Jessa had the feeling they didn't, which was surprising. Although a lake-people like this had no reason to travel far. They had all they needed here.

'It's fitting you came tonight,' the woman was saying. 'Tomorrow is the feast of giving; the opening of the darkness. We'd be honoured if you would join us.'

'If the food is as good as this,' Skapti said drily, 'I'm sure we will.'

They all laughed, and there was an awkward silence.

Then the Speaker leaned forward. 'So you're travel-

115

ling. From beyond the Wood, by the look of you. And where do you travel to, may we know?'

Skapti shot a look at Brochael, who shrugged.

'A long way,' the poet said, carefully.

'To my country.' Kari's voice was unexpected; the shaman turned to him. A strange look passed between them.

Then the Speaker nodded. 'A long way indeed, to the land of the Soul Thieves.'

Jessa caught her breath. So he knew, at least.

Kari nodded but said nothing. He drank from his cup.

A woman came in and spoke to the chieftain; he turned to Skapti. 'A guest-hall is ready for you all; Sif will show you the way. Sleep well, sleep late. Rest and eat well. Tomorrow we will talk.'

'Tomorrow we should leave,' Brochael said uneasily. 'We have an urgent errand.'

The old man shook his head. 'I fear the weather will keep you here. But the choice is yours. Do exactly as you wish. We will sell you food and ale and grain, as much as you want.'

Awkwardly Brochael stood, and nodded. 'We appreciate that.'

The guest-hall was a copy of the other, but smaller. Equally smoky, Jessa thought irritably. 'It's a wonder these people can breathe,' she said aloud.

Hakon fingered the brightly-woven hangings and lifted one aside. 'Furs!' He flung himself down with a groan of comfort.

Jessa crawled scornfully into the next booth and dumped her bag. She lay down, just for a moment, to try out the bed.

In seconds she was asleep.

116

Kari lay in the darkness. Slowly, the absence of feeling came to him. He saw nothing, heard nothing.

But there was a tightness about his neck; he put his hands up and felt for it, and touched rope, a great noose of frayed, damp rope. Desperately he pulled at it, but it was coiled and cabled with heavy knots, and something crisp, like feathers, were stuck and threaded into its skeins.

He spread his hands out into the darkness, fighting down fear. This was no dream, he knew that. It was a vision. But of what? Terror touched him; he tried to sit up, and couldn't, and then he knew the darkness on top of him was heavy, wet with peat and matted lichens and the seeds and spores of generations. It weighed on him, suffocating him like a dark hand over his mouth and nose, and though he writhed and struggled and flung his head from side to side she would not let go of him; she was drowning him in soil, her hand forcing him down and down.

He choked and retched and the darkness broke; it shattered into glints of candle-flame and a fire-red roof, and Jessa and Moongarm, bending over him.

'Are you all right?' Jessa hissed anxiously. She pulled him up, knowing he wasn't; he was white, his lips a strange blue; he struggled to breathe, bent over, dragging in long, painful, choking breaths.

'Shall I call Brochael?'

He shook his head. After a moment he managed, 'No . . . I'm . . . all right.'

'You don't look it.'

'I . . . will be.' He looked at Moongarm.

'You seemed to be stifling in your sleep,' the grey man said, sombrely.

'He woke me,' Jessa whispered. 'He was worried. Was it a nightmare?'

'I hope so.'

'A warning?'

Kari shrugged, rubbing his throat with thin fingers. 'I don't know. They seem friendly.'

'Very friendly,' Moongarm muttered.

Jessa glanced at him. 'You don't trust that?'

'I'm wary. The comfort here will be hard to leave. And if your errand is so urgent, you should beware of that.'

Kari looked up at them suddenly. 'There's one thing I do know about them, and that's strange enough.'

'What?'

He coughed, and swallowed, painfully. Then he said, 'They were expecting us. They knew we were coming.'

16

Chess in the court and cheerful.

The old man had been right.

They woke late, to a blizzard that howled around the village all morning, blotting out even the wall of the nearest house in a storm of white driven flakes. Travel was impossible. Hakon took one look outside and went back to sleep. He had a lot to catch up on, he said.

Jessa and Kari played Hunt the King on a board made by scratching out the squares with a knife. Kari did it; he was clever at carving. For counters they used some of Brochael's coins. The chieftain's daughter Lenna, who brought breakfast, stayed in the house to watch, fascinated. Jessa explained the rules.

Brochael had nothing to do. His shoulder no longer bothered him; he prowled restlessly for a while, and then pulled on his bearskin coat and went out, into the flying snow.

'Where's he gone?' Skapti muttered absently.

'To look at the horses. What else is there?' Moongarm was sharpening his sword with a long whetstone borrowed from the villagers. He gazed curiously across at the poet, who lay on a bench, wrapped in his blue cloak. Skapti had the kantele out and had tuned it carefully, adjusting the harpstrings and checking the birchwood frame for damage. Now he plucked notes with his supple fingers.

Jessa looked up from the board. 'Out of practice?'

He grinned at her. 'A feast needs a song. Even from visitors.' He looked at Lenna. 'You must have poets of your own. Storytellers? Remembers?'

She looked confused, her long black hair swinging. 'The Speaker. He knows the past.'

'Is he a shaman?'

The girl nodded, reluctant. She pushed back her hair nervously and gathered the dishes. Skapti let the notes fade. Then he said, 'I have a good song of thanks for hospitality. Would they let me sing it tonight?'

Lenna paused, her head bent. 'I don't know ... It's not that sort of feast.' Kari raised his head and looked at her quickly, and she scrambled up. 'I'd better go. My mother will want me.'

They watched her hurry across the hazy room, the brilliant reds and blues of her dress delighting their eyes. She pulled on her coat and went out.

'She was scared,' Jessa said. 'Now why was that?'

Kari moved a piece. 'Skapti's song. The prospect of hearing it.'

Jessa giggled, but wondered what he really thought.

The skald ignored them. He wrapped his cloak tight around him and leaned back against the wall. 'Don't disturb me. I'll be working.'

Then he closed his eyes and was still.

Jessa had seen him do this before. Making the song; fitting the words and notes and kennings together; knotting them into intricate lines and rhythms, charging them with power, memorizing them

120

– it was an intense, concentrated process. He would lie there now as if in a sleep for hours, with just the soft touch of a finger on a string now and then to remind them he was alive; later he would begin the music, working out patterns of sound to weave with the words.

For a long time the room was quiet. Just the click of the moving coins, the whirr of the whetstone.

Then Brochael stormed in, scattering snow. He stamped it from his boots, looking more cheerful. 'It's clearing up. I've been buying supplies from the old man – they're surprisingly generous.' He dumped three sacks in a corner. 'We should be able to leave tomorrow.'

From his bed, Hakon groaned.

Jessa laughed; she knew what he meant. The warmth, the food, the chance to rest were enticing. And just being indoors without having the eternal wind and sleet in her face, chapping her skin, stinging her eyes; without the constant stumble of the horses, the stiff, freezing nights. But they had to keep on. Signi was depending on them. She thought suddenly of the slim girl asleep in the dim room, her hair spread. Wulfgar too; by now he must be aching with worry.

'I could show you how things are there,' a voice said, 'If you want.'

She looked up at Kari, startled and furious. 'Don't do that to me!'

He looked down. 'I'm sorry, Jessa.'

'It's too dangerous . . .'

He shook his head, bitterly. 'You don't need to tell me. But sometimes, I can't help it. That picture of Signi was so strong.'

Something in his look calmed her down. Grudgingly she said, 'Show me then.'

He cleared the pieces from the table and carefully poured water from the jug the girl had left. It spread, making a thin pool.

After only a moment Jessa saw images drift on its surface. She saw the Jarlshold; it looked quiet, eerily empty. Smoke came only from two – no, three – houses, and from the hall, where glimmers of light showed in the high windows. Snow lay everywhere, blanketing the roofs, piled high against the doors, almost untrodden, as if no-one was there to venture out. On the fjordshore the ships bobbed in a line. Deserted.

Then the water seeped through the cracks of the table and drained away.

'Where are they all?'

'Inside. Those that are left.' He looked up at her strangely. 'Did you see anyone?'

'No. That's what's worrying.'

For a moment he didn't reply. Then he said, 'I did. I saw their souls, Jessa. Almost half the people now. Wandering between the houses, wrapped in their dreams like mist. They're lost. Her spell has them – even here I can feel it, feel her.'

She nodded grimly. 'She knows we're coming.'

'Of course she knows. She wants us . . . me. The closer we come to her the more I can feel her delight. And the more scared I am.'

'Why?' she asked quietly.

'Because I don't know what to do.' His voice was low, strained. 'You're all depending on me to release Signi, but I don't know how. And I don't want to see her . . . Gudrun. I don't want to see her.'

122

He looked so distraught that Brochael had come over and was listening.

'We'll worry about that when we get there,' he said gruffly. 'If I find the witch I'll know what to do.'

Kari shook his head. 'Swords are useless. You know that.'

In the afternoon the snow stopped. Jessa and Hakon went outside and explored the settlement thoroughly; no-one seemed to mind.

The sky was iron-grey, the lake frozen hard. They skittered flat stones across it, watching them ring and rattle and slither to a stop far out on the ice. Already the sun was low, a sullen red circle. Geese flew across it, honking.

'A good bow would get one,' Hakon muttered, staring up.

The village was busy with its secret preparations. It was also very well-defended, Jessa thought. The timber wall around it was higher than a man, and only two wharves jutted out, where several frail wicker and skin boats were drawn up out of the ice-grip. The only other way in was the causeway, and that was guarded at both ends.

They wandered out onto it, slipping on the frozen logs. In the marsh, men were bending. They saw the shaman rise from among the bulrushes and see them. He came over, smiling.

'What are you doing?' Jessa asked, curious.

'Preparing.' He waved the carved wand at the sky and its bells chinked. 'The weather is better. Tomorrow you'll be able to leave, if you want.'

'We will,' Jessa said firmly. 'Though you've been very kind to us. It was a godsend, finding you.'

He looked at her, his eyes amused. 'For us too, lady, it was a godsend. The dark mother brought you.'

He touched his lip, in that strange way they did, and walked along the causeway. Then he turned, abruptly.

'One question. Your friend, with the pale hair. He's a sorcerer?'

They gazed at each other. Jessa said, 'Not exactly. He . . . can do certain things.'

The Speaker nodded, smiling. 'I knew it. He and I have that in common. He has the look of one who speaks to the dark.'

The feast began when the last edge of the sun closed up and died; darkness came instantly. The villagers and their guests, all unarmed, watched it from the wharf, then they all walked in silence to the hall. There was no music, no singing.

Inside, the room was cold. They sat around the walls on benches; the hearth in the centre dark and unlit, stacked with fresh logs.

No-one spoke.

Jessa glanced at Brochael who raised his eyebrows at her; this was like no feast she had ever seen. Uneasy, she became aware of a sound, a low humming, and realized the people were making it; it grew, slow and ominous, and then they began to beat their hands, pounding out one rhythm.

The Speaker came forward. He wore a green shirt open at the neck; she saw the coiling tattoos that covered his chest and forearms, and now he cupped his hands together and crouched low, whispering and rocking to himself.

The beating rose to a climax; then stopped, instantly.

A flame had appeared, within the man's hands; the people murmured in awe. He carried it carefully through the silence to the kindling; a fire grew, steadying to red. Around her the people began to sing; a high, excited chant, with words she didn't know.

Kari can do this, she thought. But she was beginning to feel uneasy; the ritual was unfamiliar, and unnerving.

The fire grew. Red light and smoke gathered in the hall. It lit eyes and faces and hands. Blood-light, she thought.

Servers came quickly and brought everyone bowls, small wooden bowls. All empty.

'Hardly a feast,' Skapti muttered.

'I don't like this,' she said. 'Something's wrong.'

'It's too late to get out now.'

They were passing round a great board, and on the board was a cake, a huge, round thing, cut into thin wedges, one for everyone. The people took a slice each, gravely, almost reluctantly, placing it in their bowl. No-one ate it. The travellers, puzzled, did the same.

The room was full of strange, unspoken tension.

When everyone had been served, the Speaker stood by the new fire, wand in hand. He raised it slightly, and the crystals and bells glinted with fiery hearts.

'Dark one,' he said, his voice low, 'you give and you take. Now, in the time of the sun's death, choose the one you will have.'

He nodded.

The people, reluctantly, began to eat.

Uneasy, Jessa looked at the others. Suddenly she felt afraid. She did not want to touch the cake; a rich crumbling mass of oatflour and berries and fruits, but everyone else was, so she picked it up and nibbled a corner. It tasted good. Rich and honey-sweet; delicious. She ate more.

People were looking round, watching their neighbours. Beside her, Skapti coughed; then he coughed again, almost choking. Hastily she slapped his back; he retched and spat something into his hand.

It was a large hazel nut, baked hard as stone.

They stared at it, astonished.

And in that moment everyone moved. Jessa was grabbed, forced still. The Speaker had a sharp knife at Skapti's chest – two other men held him from the back.

'So it's you,' the Speaker breathed, his eyes bright. 'She's chosen you, poet.'

Hakon was struggling; Moongarm and Brochael held tight. No-one touched Kari, but they surrounded him where he sat, white with shock.

'Do something!' Jessa screamed, struggling. 'Kari!'

'I'd be grateful,' Skapti breathed, trying to smile.

'I can't.' Kari was amazed. 'I can't reach him.'

The Speaker grinned at her. 'I have a spell about me, lady. I told you he and I had things in common.'

17

Oaths were broken, binding vows,
Solemn agreements sworn between them.

The guest-hall was their prison now. Each of them
was bound firmly, hand and foot, with ropes of hemp.
Where Skapti had been taken none of them knew;
the villagers had dragged him from the hall. He had
been silent and dignified, with only a quick, hopeless
glance at the others. Now the Speaker came in and
looked down at them all. His eyes were bright, his
face flushed. But his words came clear enough.

'I regret it had to be your friend; there's never
any way of knowing. You won't be harmed, any
of you. Tomorrow, when the giving is over, you can
go.'

'Where's Skapti?' Brochael roared. 'What are you
doing with him?'

The shaman looked at him gravely. 'The darkness
will eat him.'

He glanced at Kari. 'As for you, enchanter, I've
made sure you can't harm me, and I'll be with him
from now until the end. If there's any disturbance,
any hint of trouble, I'll kill him at once. Do you
understand?'

Kari nodded, unhappily.

The Speaker turned and went out. They heard the door being bolted behind him.

Silence hung heavy around them. Finally Moongarm broke it.

'They'll kill him anyway, and it won't be a clean death.'

Brochael shook his head. 'I've heard of this,' he said heavily. 'The victim is chosen by chance – whoever gets the sacred seed, or whatever. Skapti would know more. They'd say the earth-mother chose him. Then they give him to her – I don't know how.'

'I do.' Kari leaned his head back against the wall. 'They'll take him to the bog, tie a garrotte about his throat and choke him – but not to death. Then they throw him in.'

Aghast, Jessa said, 'Is that what you dreamed?'

He nodded. 'I didn't know what it meant till now.'

'But when? How much time have we got?'

'I don't know.'

'They might be doing it now,' Hakon whispered.

The door-bolt slammed; they were silent, instantly. The girl Lenna came in, carrying a heavy tray of hot, steaming food. The feast must have really begun now, Jessa thought, now they all knew they were safe. Two men with spears were behind her.

She put the tray down.

'How are we supposed to eat?' Hakon asked.

She looked at him. 'I'll untie one hand for each of you – the left. But not him.' She glanced at Kari, a frightened look.

He shrugged. 'I'm not hungry.'

She undid the ropes very carefully, keeping well back. They looked at the food but no-one had any appetite.

128

Then Brochael reached out. 'Eat it,' he ordered. 'We need to be ready for anything. Starving won't help.'

The girl crouched by the fire, putting on wood. The flamelight shone on her glossy hair, the thin fox outlined on her face.

Jessa said, 'Don't you care about him?'

The girl paused, her hands sticky from the fresh logs. Then she went on piling them up. 'It will be for the best,' she said, in a low voice. 'His blood will enrich the land. He'll nurture our crops; feed our cattle. Because of him the dark one will be pleased.'

Jessa felt rage swelling in her; she wanted to shake the girl and scream at her. 'But he's not one of your people!' she yelled. 'He belongs with us, and we came here as guests, we trusted you! You lied to us . . .'

'No.'

'. . . yes! Lied! And now you'll murder him!'

'Not murder . . . no.' The girl shook her head hastily.

'And he had no say,' Hakon said, watching her closely. 'He didn't know. None of us did.'

'He has to do it!' Lenna jumped up, her eyes wide with terror. 'If he doesn't it will be one of us, don't you see? One of us! And everyone is so happy now, so relieved. Every year this terror comes round . . . if the dark one isn't given her choice there is famine, death, disease. It's for the best. I'm sorry. But it's for the best.'

She hurried to the door, saying to the guards, 'Tie them up. Quickly.'

'Wait.' Jessa looked up. 'One question.'

The girl did not turn.

'When will it be?'

Lenna paused, her hand on the door. The long ends of her hair swung down and hid her face; her dress swished around the soft boots she wore.

'Dawn,' she said. Then she opened the door and went out.

They waited till the men had tied up their hands and left before anyone spoke again.

'Neatly done,' Moongarm looked at Jessa and Hakon. 'Quite a team.'

'I can't do anything with the ropes,' Kari said simply. 'There's some sorcery about them – they won't burn or untie for me. Someone else will have to untie us.'

'Where are the birds?' Jessa asked.

'Outside. They can't get in.'

'Even if we could get free,' Moongarm pointed out from his corner, 'how could we leave the village? There's a man outside, and the only way off is across the causeway. That will be guarded. So will the skald.'

'You seem keen to point out difficulties,' Brochael muttered. 'Can't you do anything else?'

'These are truths, tawny man.'

'There's another way out.' Jessa had had an idea; her face lit with thought. 'Listen Kari, we have to get free, but not yet. After all they may look in on us. It needs to be just before dawn. Is there anything you can do then?'

He smiled at her sideways. 'Oh, I can do something, Jessa. No matter what the Speaker says.'

It was difficult, in the dim room, to keep track of time. The night seemed endless. Outside the wind had dropped; the faint sounds of voices and music

130

drifted from the hall. Later a drum began, just one, a low muffled beat like a pulse from somewhere nearby. Kari recognized it; he had heard it before, like a warning. They all lay awake listening to it; a shaman's drum, like the beat of a heart. They came to wait for each beat, dreading it, yet fearing it would stop. Lying in the dark Hakon thought it was the beat of Skapti's heart, and he wondered in what hut the thin poet was lying, and if he had guessed what was happening to him. Knowing Skapti, he had. And he must know they wouldn't desert him. Hakon smiled, sadly. The skald's acid remarks had cheered him up many a time; his sly teasing, his songs, his endless, useless knowledge. Already, they were missing Skapti.

Finally, Moongarm, who had some strange instinct about time, told them it was near dawn. Jessa sat up, restless. 'Right. We go now.'

Each of them looked at Kari, not knowing what to expect. But he sat against the wall, unmoving.

'What can you do?' Hakon asked at last.

'Quiet!' Brochael growled. 'Look!'

The door was being unbarred, quietly and smoothly, from the outside. A figure slid around it, well muffled against the cold. It was the guard. He leaned his spear against the wall and came forward; they saw his eyes were wide with terror.

'Don't make me do this,' he pleaded, hoarsely. 'How can you be here in my mind?'

'I'm sorry.' Kari shifted from the wall. 'I have no choice.'

The man bent; despite his own will his hands went to the ropes about Kari's wrists.

131

'Hurry up!' Jessa said, 'or they'll notice he's missing!'

When they were all untied the man stood still, as if Kari had forbidden him to move. His eyes watched them as they gathered their belongings, buckled on belts and weapons, picked up the sacks of supplies.

'Now,' Kari said to him gently. 'Outside.'

At the door he picked up his spear again; Hakon looked out, cautiously. 'No-one about.'

In the snow the man bolted the door and stood against it. Even in the cold he was sweating. Kari reached out and touched him lightly, once, on the forehead.

'I'm sorry,' he said again.

Then he turned and walked away, between the houses. The others followed; they paused in the shadow of a wall.

'Will he remember?' Jessa whispered.

'No. When they find us gone he'll be as surprised as the rest.' He sounded disgusted with himself. Moongarm looked at him with a strange respect. 'I fear you more than them, Kari.'

Kari glared at him, his eyes cold as frost. 'So you should,' he said, bitterly.

The village was silent; held in frozen night. Only the drum still beat, an ominous reminder of time passing. Jessa led them to the wharves; there she crouched down and nodded out onto the lake.

'That's our way off.'

'The ice!' Moongarm raised his eyebrows. 'Ingenious. But will it bear our weight?'

'I don't know but it's our only way off this island.'

'And Skapti?'

'We wait until they bring him, at the bog. We'll see them coming. Then we attack.'

'Yes, but the horses!' Hakon was aghast. 'We can't leave them!'

There was silence. Each of them knew they could never get the horses out without rousing the entire village.

'It's a heavy choice,' Brochael said grimly, 'but Jessa's right, this is the only way. I think we're on foot from now on.'

They climbed down over the edge of the wharf to the timbers beneath. Jessa stepped off first, carefully. The dawn cold was bitter; her breath clouded and froze on her knotted scarves. The lake lay before her, a rigid, shimmering mirror, white under the crescent moon, with the long blue shadows of the buildings stretching across it.

The night was silent. Stars glittered, clear and hard.

As she put her toe on the ice she felt the coldness underfoot, expected the slab to tip, to crack, but although her growing weight made strange wheezing sounds deep under the surface, it stayed solid. She stepped out and stood still, her footsteps ringing.

'It's thick.'

Carefully, testing every step, she walked out into the lake, the others slipping behind her. In the hard frost every step and creak sounded loud, every slither enormous. She found herself holding her breath, and let it out in a cloud of mist. Every moment she expected the crack; the darkness underneath to open and swallow her. And why not, because it was the darkness they were defying; the darkness that wanted Skapti.

'You won't get him,' she thought. Looking back

133

she saw the others; Kari was light, and Hakon too. But Brochael was taking careful steps, as if he feared his own weight would bring him down. Silent and surefooted, Moongarm was a grey shape under the moon.

Half-way over, she heard voices. Lights flared on the causeway.

She crouched, hearing Hakon slither up beside her. 'Brochael says hurry. They're coming out.'

She nodded, and crawled on, keeping on hands and knees now, until the plate of ice under her wet glove suddenly shifted, and she stopped. 'It's the edge.'

'Be careful, Jessa!'

They were already among the rushes, on the edge of the bog. Here the ice thinned to a lace-fine fringe which crackled and splintered under her. Then her feet were in brown brackish water, knee-deep, the reeds high above her.

'Why doesn't it freeze?' she breathed.

'I don't know and I don't want to know,' Brochael growled, out of the dark. 'Keep to the edge. It'll be treacherous further in.'

They waded through the ice-cold muck, working their way round to the causeway. Once Hakon's foot went deep and he staggered; Moongarm hauled him out, silently. Shadows among the reeds, they crouched and watched the torches approach from the village. The stink of stagnant rotting growth hung about them.

A small group were crossing the causeway.

'How many?' Brochael said.

'Four.'

134

Behind, well-back, the villagers stood, as if they dared come no nearer.

'Where is he?'

'In front,' Moongarm murmured. 'With the Speaker.'

She saw him then, his thin, upright figure, that lanky walk. They had taken his coat off; his shirt was open and about his neck was a great noose of hemp, knotted strangely. He was silent, maybe gagged. He was alert though, she thought. He was probably wondering where they were.

But Skapti knew exactly where they were. He also knew what was happening; as Brochael had guessed, he had heard of such things before. And as he stumbled on, pushed from behind and shivering with cold and fear, he tugged and twisted his bound wrists uselessly to red sores until the voice spoke, quietly inside his mind.

'Get ready, Skapti. You weren't afraid we would leave you?'

He grinned, unable to help it.

The voice had been Kari's.

The Speaker and his prisoner and two torch-bearers came right on into the swampy ground, the morass of clotted peat and moss squelching under them.

'Ready,' Brochael whispered.

Each of them had their weapons to hand; Hakon gripped his sword tight.

'Here's your chance to name that,' Jessa breathed.

He wondered how she could joke; his own chest was tight with tension.

'I'll take the Speaker,' Brochael said. 'You two, the others. Jessa, get Skapti.' He looked at Kari.

'You'll have to deal with the rest – the people on the causeway. If they cross . . .'

'Leave them to me.' The ravens had come down; one was perched on his shoulder, gripping the dark cloth with its great talons.

'What will you do?'

'Keep them back.'

'Yes, but how?'

'Like this.'

As he said it the night seemed to crack open. The Speaker spun around as a white gate of searing flame leapt up to bar the causeway; it spat and sparked like lightening. People screamed.

'Now!' Brochael hissed.

They leapt out, yelling, flinging the torchbearers aside, the flames falling and hissing out in the black water.

The Speaker cried out something in rage; Jessa saw him turn at her, but Hakon was there; he sliced the air with his sword between them and the shaman jerked back, stumbled, twisted away from Brochael's axe. He fell, full-length, floundering in the black ooze.

Jessa grabbed Skapti, sliced his bonds. 'It's us!'

He grinned. 'Thought you'd abandoned me.'

'Not us.'

As she turned she thought the Speaker would be up, but he wasn't; instead she saw the marsh was bubbling and churning around him, and a blackness seemed to rise and gather from it, covering him as he screamed and struggled, bending over him, a dark form. His voice choked, broke, bubbled. Half a cry hung endlessly on the silent air.

Skapti grabbed her arm. 'Come on!'

As they fled the sudden silence behind chilled them; only Kari's fire-gate crackled under the moon, the people behind it watching, without a sound.

Along the road they raced, into the darkness, laden with packs and weapons, always looking back. Snow, deeper than before, slowed them, and then, just ahead, they heard the howl of wolves; a pack, hungry.

Jessa stopped dead, the others slamming into her.

'Get up the hill,' Moongarm yelled. 'Leave these to me.' He flung his pack at Hakon and drew his sword.

'Not alone,' Brochael growled.

But the man was gone, transformed suddenly to shadow.

Kari turned away. 'Let him go. Come on!'

Uphill they raced, to a stand of pines that rose in a dark line against the stars. Once there they leaned against the trees, gasping for breath.

The rune-gate still burned below; the searing light from it crackling above the lake. But Kari was looking elsewhere, at the wolves hurtling after them up the slope; at least ten, low, misty shapes.

'Give me my sword!' Skapti yelled.

'You won't need it.' Kari pointed. 'Look down there.'

A grey shape sat waiting on the hillside. It too was a wolf, but larger than any Jessa had ever seen, and it sat as still as a stone under the stars. Its amber eyes glinted in the rune-light.

The wolf-pack saw it. They slowed, stopped, yelping.

Then one by one they slunk away from it, in terror.

18

The wolf is loose.

Miles away and hours later, huddled under an over-hang of rock, the travellers watched the sun strengthen.

They were silent, breathless from the long scramble into the hills, and from fascinated, uneasy curiosity. No-one wanted to ask the question; it was Hakon who finally couldn't bear it any more.

He turned to Moongarm, abruptly. 'That wolf,' he said, clenching his hand nervously. 'What was it?'

The grey man stared at him, expressionless. 'Just a wolf. It came from nowhere. A pack leader, I would say. The others seemed to slink off when they saw it.'

His amber eyes challenged them all, levelly. Then he went back to eating the villagers' bread.

Hakon turned a bewildered look on Jessa. She glanced at Brochael.

The big man was glaring at Moongarm, his face set with a grim, hostile fear. 'So where did it go?' he asked harshly, 'this convenient wolf? Does it still follow us? Has it been with us all along?'

The man did not turn. 'It went into the dark,' he said, quietly.

Brochael was livid; Jessa knew Moongarm's cool-

138

ness made him want to explode with rage. It was only Kari's urgent shake of the head that kept him silent. Intrigued, she kicked snow from her boots. So the man was a shape-shifter. A were-man. All of them seemed to have guessed that now, and all of them, she thought dryly, were terrified of it. Except perhaps Kari. You never knew what Kari was thinking. And she liked Moongarm, had come to like him. He was quiet, watchful, yes, but shy, a man with a great secret. Now they knew what it was. And he obviously wasn't going to explain anything.

'At least,' Skapti said quietly, 'we're all alive.'

'Without the horses,' Hakon said.

'There was no help for that. And I have to say I'm grateful to all of you for getting my neck out of that noose. Especially Jessa.' He put a long arm round her shoulders and squeezed her. She grinned.

'Kari made the fire-gate.'

He nodded.

'I know you wouldn't have worried,' Brochael said gruffly. 'Not with your courage.'

Jessa giggled.

'Thank you,' Skapti said lazily. 'I was, of course, terrified. And did you also know, or haven't you worked it out in your snail-shell of a brain yet, that I wasn't chosen by any earth-goddess, but by the shaman?'

They all stared at him. Only Kari nodded.

'The ravenmaster has, I see.' Skapti sat up, rubbing his cold hands together. 'They knew we were coming, didn't they – the Speaker knew. So we were a god-send. He made sure one of us would be the gift to their earth-hunger. I had plenty of time tied up in that hut to work it out. He chose me, probably because he thought I was the cleverest.' He grinned. 'They didn't know about Jessa.'

'So they knew where the seed was?' Hakon said. 'In which piece?'

'Not all of them. He knew.'

'And what about afterwards? That thing in the marsh, that dragged him in . . .'

For a moment they all saw it again, the dark bubbling of the peaty water.

'Ah, now. That's beyond me.' Skapti sat back. 'Kari's the one for spirits and earth-wraiths. Something came out of there for him, that's sure enough. Something out of the dark.'

They sat silent, thinking about it. Then Brochael sighed, and reached for his pack. 'Let's get on.' He glanced at Moongarm, as if to say something. Then he turned away.

Already they were high in the foothills, the snow here deep under a frozen crust. As they travelled north all vestige of the giants' road was lost; they waded up bare white slopes, leaving a blue tear of shadow; through gloomy stunted firs whitened with thick snow-falls, frosted into place.

The cold became intense; the daylight always shorter. For two days they struggled over the high passes, stumbling and falling and pulling each other up, soaked and shivering, trying to keep the food-sacks dry. Their lungs ached with the tingling air. Without Kari's rune-fires they would have frozen; as it was each night was an ordeal of cold, a quest for kindling and a place out of the raw winds that seared the exposed skin about their eyes. The world had turned white, had become an endless tilted plateau, and they seemed always to be climbing, their toes and ears and fingers raw with pain.

On the second night a blizzard swept down; a howling fury of stinging ice that drove them into the only shelter they could find, a narrow cleft where all of them huddled together shivering, the ravens perched mournfully above. There was no fire; Kari had sunk into sleep at once and none of them had the heart to wake him, but at least they were out of the eternal wind.

One by one, the others drifted off to sleep.

Jessa couldn't; she was shivering, and the rough knobbly floor stuck into her back. She shifted, restless.

'Awake?' Brochael murmured.

'Too cold.'

'Come closer.'

She moved against him, and he put his great arm around her, just as his left held Kari. 'Better?'

She tugged the blanket close. 'You're warmer than the floor.'

'That's not saying much.'

For a moment they were silent; then she whispered, 'Brochael, do you think we'll get through?'

'Of course we will.' His voice was gruff. 'They're depending on us.'

There was no doubt about that.

'Still . . .' she murmured.

'I'll tell you what worries me more than the snow, Jessa. It's that were-creature we're dragging with us, like a shadow. What does he want? What sort of a thing is he?'

They both watched Moongarm's lean huddle in the corner; he slept silently, breathing deep.

'He's one of us now,' she said.

'Oh no! He'd like to be. But I'll never have that – I'll never trust him, not until I know where he's going and why, and how this curse came on him. A man who can slither into wolf-shape is no fellow-traveller for me. He could turn on any of us. Is he man or animal?'

'Kari is more than a match for him,' Jessa murmured, sleepily.

When he didn't answer she opened her eyes, surprised. 'Don't you think so?'

'Kari sometimes worries me more.'

She sat up then and looked at him. In the pale shimmer of the reflected snow all the russet of his hair and beard seemed drained from him; he looked thinner, with a gather of lines between his eyebrows.

'Why?' she whispered.

He looked at her. 'Jessa, where are we going? To Gudrun, if we get there. To some land of sorcery and soul-theft that's not even in this world. And all the time I can feel him gathering himself, summoning all the skill and mind-craft that's in him. His mind is often away, somehow – back in the Jarlshold, talking to ghosts and spirits and the birds . . . I don't know where. I'm afraid of what it's doing to him.'

She shook her head. 'He's done this before, the fire-gate . . .'

'Oh lights and fires, that's nothing. It's the rest. The outlaw. That guard.'

She pulled a face. 'Moving minds?'

He nodded, wondering. 'Imagine the power of that, Jessa, the secret, tingling power! Making everyone around you do just what you want. And they – we – would never know.'

'He won't. He wouldn't.' Jessa settled back firmly.

'He may have to. To defeat Gudrun he may have to become like her. Almost certainly, he will have to kill her.'

Appalled, she stared at him. On his other side Kari twisted in his sleep, the long hair falling from his eyes.

'Or she him,' Brochael murmured.

In the morning they went on, weak from cold. It froze on their eyebrows and lashes; all the brief afternoon the snow fell, relentless. Only after nightfall did the sky clear, and reveal the breath-catching steely glitter of millions of stars, the aurora shimmering over them.

By the third day the travellers were worn to numbness. They were high in the mountains, a place of bare rock, frozen, icy chasms and passes; clattering rockfalls and the eternal howling wind. They rarely spoke now, ploughing on in a straggling group, their thoughts wandering, lost in their own pain and hunger. There was only snow to drink; they gathered handfuls and sucked it. The food from the village was almost gone, and Brochael handed it out rarely.

Jessa's eyes ached from the snow-glare; her lips were chapped, windsores chafed her face. Hakon was limping badly, perhaps with frost-bite, but he kept up and said nothing.

They hardly knew that the land had begun to descend beneath their feet; they reached the treeline with a vague recognition, and trudged wearily in under the frost-stiff branches.

Kari stumbled and fell. For a moment he did not get up, and Brochael went back and bent over him.

When they caught up with the others the big man said, 'Time to rest.' His voice was hoarse with cold.

Under the silent trees they sat and ate the last scraps of food. Skapti flung an empty sack away; the ravens came down and picked it over. Even they looked skeletal, Jessa thought.

With an effort she said, 'We're over the mountains.'

Brochael nodded. None of them answered; their relief was deep and unspoken. Below them broken forestry descended into the snow-filled glacier. On the horizon faint fog drifted. Hakon stared at it through red-rimmed eyes, and roused himself. 'Is that smoke?'

'Could be. Could be just mist.'

Brochael glanced at Kari, who shrugged. 'I can't tell,' he murmured.

Jessa looked at him. He looked bone-weary, and frail as ice, but his pale skin and hair fitted here; he belonged, more than any of them. And the further north they went, the deeper into frosts and whiteness and sorcery, the more he seemed to have a strength that the rest of them lacked; a power, not in his body, but deeper. He was a Snow-walker, she thought suddenly.

By the next day, weak with hunger, they had come to the region of smoke. It had not faded, or blown away, and now Brochael thought there was too much of it to be a settlement.

As they journeyed towards it over the bleak tundra the air changed, became warmer; a strange dry breeze sprang up. Jessa pulled the frozen scarf from

144

her hair and scratched, wearily, looking ahead. Surely the land was grey; bare of snow.

'What are we coming to?'

Behind her, Skapti shifted the kantele on his bony shoulders. 'Musphelheim.'

'What?'

'The land of fire. Or to be exact, Jessa, a volcano.'

19

Fumes reek, into flames burst,
The sky itself is scorched with fire.

The volcano probably saved their lives.

Jessa realized that, standing knee-deep in the grey, bubbling mud, the incredible warmth thawing her toes and legs. It was wonderful.

All around her the ground bubbled and heaved, puffing up globules that burst with strange, popping sounds; insects whined around them. The air stank of sulphur and unknown, steamy gases, but it was warm, even hot in places. Bizarre plants grew here; things she'd never seen before, and birds too, flew in flocks over the warm land.

Standing next to her like a long-legged stork, his boots around his neck, Skapti was studying the map.

'Not much marked. We could be here, I suppose.' His finger touched a faded rune in the sealskin, on the far side of the mountains. Neither of them could read it.

Jessa looked at the emptiness above it. The great gash of Ginnungagap was all that was left.

'We're getting close,' she said.

'We need to.' Skapti rolled the map. 'Time's going on.' He sighed, blissfully, as if he was wriggling his invisible toes in the volcanic heat. 'Flame-tongue, Loki-land, dwarves furnace. Matter for poetry.'

'It would be if we had something to eat.'

'Animals will come here. We'll set snares.'

They had made camp on the edge of the lava-field; the rock there was contorted and twisted, forced from the earth hot. Cinders littered the soil; tiny plants sprouted between them. On the opposite side of the valley the snow still lay.

Kari sat by the fire, his coat off, watching the steams and mists churn from the mud. Hakon lay beside him, eyes closed.

Skapti took one look at Brochael and said, 'What's wrong?' The big man sat wrathfully cleaning his axe with a lump of pumice, each stroke a slice of anger. It was Kari who answered.

'Moongarm has gone hunting.'

'Good! So?'

Kari nudged the grey man's pack with his foot. They saw the hilt of the sword jutting out – Moongarm's only weapon.

'Without that?' Then Jessa understood. She sat down, thoughtfully.

'He said we needed food and that he would get it. Then he was gone, into the smoke.'

'If he thinks I'll eat any of that . . . filth,' Brochael burst out.

'You must.' Skapti sat down, his knees pulled up. 'Signi and Wulfgar – all of them – are depending on us. We eat, Brochael. Even wolf-carrion.'

Brochael spat, but said nothing.

'While he's gone,' Jessa said, 'we should talk. Has he said anything to any of you? About what he wants?'

They all shook their heads. Hakon opened his eyes and propped himself on one elbow. 'Is he safe?'

Kari shook his head. 'Not altogether. He becomes an animal, in body, perhaps in mind. There are sudden surges of wildness about him.'

'And that means sorcery,' Skapti put in.

'No.' Kari shook his head. 'Not of his own.'

'Well I don't care whose!' Brochael said fiercely. 'We watch him! All the time!'

It was late, just before dawn, when Moongarm reappeared. Hakon was awake, and he saw the lean figure stride suddenly out of the sulphurous fogs and rumbling red glows of the lava-field.

Moongarm squatted by the fire. His eyes were bright, with a wild, satisfied look in them that Hakon avoided. When he spoke his voice was rasping and hoarse.

'Cook this. Wake the others when it's ready.'

He flung down a dripping carcase, already skinned and gutted. What it was Hakon wasn't sure – it looked like goat. Feeling briefly like a thrall again he prepared it. For a while the were-man stayed there and watched him, lazily, by the fire. Finally it made Hakon uneasy.

'Stop staring at me,' he muttered.

Moongarm grinned. 'Bothers you, doesn't it.'

Spitting the meat, Hakon glanced up. The man's lips were drawn back; his sharp teeth gleamed. Blood was on his hands and clothing.

Hakon put his hand on his sword.

Moongarm laughed then, and stood up. 'Don't wake me,' he murmured. 'I've already eaten.'

The smell of the cooking meat woke Jessa; once she realized what it was she sat up quickly and stared

148

across. Hakon was turning it on a rough spit; the fat dripped into the flames, crackling and hissing. She hurried over.

'Wake the others,' he muttered. 'It's ready.'

'Moongarm's?'

'Yes.' He frowned at her. 'The gods know how he got it, Jessa.'

'I don't care,' she said, firmly.

They all ate hungrily, even Brochael, though he was unhappy and silent. It was goat, or some wild relative, although they'd seen no sign of any animals.

Behind them, Moongarm slept easily under his blanket.

Kari threw scraps to the ravens; they swooped out of the dusk and tore them up and gobbled them.

'Those birds don't look as scrawny as they did,' Skapti remarked.

'They went after Moongarm,' Kari said. 'Ate his leftovers.'

'And he was in wolf-shape?' Jessa asked quietly.

'Yes. A great grey wolf, the ravens say. His body slept and it rose from him like a wraith.'

Everyone touched their amulets; Brochael grasped the thorshammer at his neck. But no-one said anything. They didn't know what to say.

Before the weak sun rose they were moving on, trudging over the lava-field, picking out a way. To their left the ground bubbled and steamed; yellow, flung splashes of sulphur seared the rocks. The air was dry, full of fumes; it made Jessa cough.

Coming over a small rise they felt the ground tremble; they stopped, alarmed. It vibrated under their feet, as if huge pressures were building up.

'It's erupting!' Jessa hissed.

Brochael grabbed her. 'Run!'

But the floor shook, toppling them all; the noise rose to a hiss and a whistle and a scream, and suddenly it was released, and a scalding fountain of water shot straight up out of the mud into the sky. Astonished, they picked themselves up and gazed at it; their faces wet with the steam and hot droplets. Then it was gone, instantly. Far off another burst out.

'What are these?' Brochael marvelled.

'Waterspouts,' Skapti said, unpoetic for once. 'That much is clear. It must build up underneath. It's a steaming cauldron down there; the earth-forge, Hel's anvil. The crust we walk on is weak; in places it breaks.'

Crossing the lava-field took almost all day; the ground was ashen, choked with cinders, and fumes and plumes of smoke drifted from it. In places it had cracked and fallen away, and they saw in deep ravines below them the slow red magma, flowing and curling and hardening in dark, crusted clots.

Gradually, late in the afternoon, the air became cooler; they came to soil of black cinders. The rocks here were bigger; their surfaces pulverized and pitted with holes; riddled with tiny lava-tunnels. Leaning against one for breath Skapti said, 'Look there.'

It was a small circular pool of water, clear as glass. The weak sun gleamed on it, making its surface glitter.

They were all thirsty, so they scrambled towards it over the rocks. Jessa's foot slid into a crack and wedged; Kari waited for her while she tugged it out.

'I feel filthy,' she said irritably. 'Covered with dust.'

'It hangs in the air,' he said, looking up.

150

They hurried after the others, who had reached the pool and were bending over it.

A raven squawked above them; it flapped past, brushing their faces with the draught of its wings.

Kari stopped dead.

She bumped against him.

'Look,' he hissed.

Astonished, she gazed over his shoulder. Skapti and Hakon were lying still, sprawled; as she watched, Brochael crumpled and fell, the water spilling from the leather sack in his hand into the dry rocks. Moongarm lay beyond him.

Jessa clenched her fists. 'It's poisoned!'

'I don't think so.' He nodded. 'Over there.'

Jessa stared into the smoke. Slowly she made out a shape standing among its drifts and swirls; a woman, a young woman, her black hair tied back. She came forward, picking her way over and staring down at the sprawled men. Then she bent; when she stood up she had Hakon's sword in her hand. She stood over him, considering.

'No!' Jessa stepped forward. The woman turned, like an animal turns. She said something, moved her hand in some gesture, but Kari ignored it and came on, jumping down among the lava. Jessa followed.

Up close, the woman was strange. Her skin was shining with grease rubbed into it; her eyes were narrow and slanting. She wore thick furs, right up to her neck, and boots of the same, enviably warm. She stared at them both curiously.

'It won't work on me,' Kari said.

'So I see.' The woman looked down at Skapti and laughed. 'Pity. Three of my goats have been stolen.

These are the thieves, I thought.' She looked back at him. 'Do you pursue them?'

'They're our friends.'

'Are they? And why has one of the Snow-walkers crossed the rainbow?'

Kari looked at her, unmoving. The words of the wraith-soldier in the wood flickered into his mind; a glimmer of colours, a warning, a long fall into the dark.

Jessa glanced at him, then at the woman. 'Have you killed them?'

'No. I can wake them. Or your friend can.'

'We didn't mean to steal,' Kari said quietly. 'We've come a long way. We're looking for the land of the Snow-walkers.'

For a moment she looked at him, puzzled. Then she snapped her fingers; the sprawled sleepers stirred and she looked down at them scornfully.

'Get them up,' she said. 'Bring them.'

20

The old songs of men I remember best.

'She's a skraeling,' Skapti whispered. 'I've heard of them.'

From the back of the room the woman emerged, carrying cheese and fish. 'So the barbarians of the south call us,' she said, coolly.

She put the food into the sack and pushed it towards them. 'This is for you to take tomorrow. It's all I can spare.'

'Thank you,' Jessa said in surprise.

'Oh, I have a price.'

They looked at each other uneasily. The woman's dark eyes noticed; she smiled through the smoke of the fire. 'But first, tell me how you came to the ends of the earth.'

It was to Jessa she spoke, and Jessa told the story, as quickly and clearly as she could. The woman listened, sitting close to the flames, once or twice nodding her glossy hair. The smoky tallow dips that lit the small house reeked of goat-fat; they showed only shadowy corners, a loom, a scatter of skins.

'And now,' Jessa said, 'we need what you know.'

'Indeed you do.' The woman put her fingertips together. She looked at them all. 'You are a strange company, to have come so far. Beyond the wood is a land of legends.'

'As is this land for us,' Skapti said, smiling.

'So all legends are true, then. But as for what lies before you . . .' She shook her head. 'All I know is this. Two days walk to the north of here is the great chasm. Even before you see it, hours before, you will hear it, a raging of blizzards, a roaring of the elements. The wind will be a wall before you. Crossing the chasm is a bridge, a mighty structure of ice and crystals, lifted by sorcery. It comes and goes in the sky. It leads, they say, to the land of the Snow-walkers. Of that place I know nothing.'

She looked at Kari. 'But I have seen them, once or twice; glimpsed them in the blizzard. They are white as ice, and have strange powers. Like gods.'

Kari shook his head. 'Not that.'

'You should know, traveller.'

'What about you?' Jessa asked. 'Why do you live here alone?'

The woman smiled again. 'There are many of us. The others travel between sea and pasture, in the blizzards and the ice-floes, with the flocks. This is the place of memory; the place between heat and cold, light and darkness. One of us is always here. I am the memory-keeper, the story-weaver. Here I weave the happenings and hangings of my people.'

'Their history?'

'Their memory. What is a people without memory? Nothing but a whisper on the ice. Later, Jessa, I will show you, all of you.'

'But your price for the food,' Brochael growled.

She looked at them, silently. Then she said, 'I have an enemy.'

'And you want us to . . .?'

'Ask him to leave.'

'And if he won't?'

'Kill him.'

Skapti threw a worried look at Brochael.

The woman smiled, mocking. 'The idea appals you.'

'We're not murderers, nor outlaws,' Brochael said heavily. 'At least not all of us. Who is he? What has he done to you?'

She laughed, amused, and her laughter shocked them until Kari said, 'Don't tease them. Tell them what you mean.'

Touching his shoulder lightly she said, 'I mean to.' Then she lifted her eyes to Brochael. 'He knows why I laugh. This enemy of mine is not a man.'

'A woman?' Hakon was appalled.

Her dark eyes lit; she shook her head. 'Not a woman either.'

'An animal,' Moongarm said quietly.

'I thought you would know.' Spreading her hands to the blaze she said, 'Every night, in the starlight, a great bear prowls about this house. It hungers for the goats. It kills anyone that travels here. If it will not go, I would have that bear's skin.'

She looked at Kari. 'You must speak to it for me.'

Worried, Brochael said, 'Look, a bear is a danger-ous creature . . .'

'So are wraiths and ghosts and spirits. The Snow-walkers move among them, speak to them as I speak to you. Isn't this true?'

Kari nodded. 'I'll try,' he said simply.

'And if it won't go we'll do what we can,' Brochael muttered.

'You should. Or tomorrow it will be hunting you.'

Brochael stood up. 'We'll go and get things ready. Jessa, you stay here.' He flashed her a look; she knew what it meant, and sat down again, warming her hands and hiding her annoyance. The others went out; Hakon closed the door.

The woman bent closer. 'You have strange companions.'

'Some of them.'

'One is a shape-shifter, I see that. And the two bird-wraiths that sit on my roof; did you know that they are also sometimes like men, tall, cloaked in black?'

Jessa stared in surprise.

'The Snow-walker is the strangest of all. He has an emptiness deep inside; a blank space where his childhood should be.' She put both hands around herself, hugging. 'And all of you are hung about with dreams; they're snagged and caught on you, as if you had burst through a web of them.'

Jessa nodded, silent.

After a moment the woman went on, 'There is something else. Your story put me in mind of it. Many weeks ago I heard a sound in the night and opened the door of my house, just a crack. I saw a tall white woman coming north over the snow. Behind her a girl walked – a girl with fine yellow hair and a blue silken dress. They were joined, hand to hand, by a silver thread, and the thread was made of dreams. Then the moon clouded. When it passed they had gone.'

'Signi!' Jessa breathed.

'I would say so. The other one was your friend's image.'

156

Jessa nodded, gloomily, and the woman watched her. 'Be warned, Jessa. These Snow-walkers are not people like us. How can he defeat her without using the same powers as she does?'

Astonished, Jessa looked at her, remembering Brochael's fears; then the door opened and Hakon and Moongarm came in. Behind them Skapti ducked under the low doorway.

'We've tied a goat outside,' Brochael said shortly.

The woman smiled. 'I would prefer not to lose it.'

'Lady,' Skapti said, graciously, 'we'll do our best.'

The bear did not come. As night fell they lay listening, wrapped warm in furs. Brochael and Skapti discussed tactics; Hakon sharpened his sword. His hands shook a little, but Jessa knew he would forget his nerves if it came to a fight.

Moongarm said, 'What do you want me to do in this?'

'Go to sleep!'

The grey man did not smile. 'This is a bear, Brochael. You'll need all the help you can get.'

'Not yours!'

'Brochael . . .' Skapti muttered.

'No!' The big man thumped a fist, stubbornly. He glared at the were-man. 'I won't fight alongside a man I don't trust. My friends, yes, but not you. You stay here.'

For a moment Moongarm gazed at him calmly, his strange eyes unblinking. 'You're a short-sighted man, Brochael.'

'I see far enough. I see through you.'

Moongarm's eyes narrowed, but he said nothing. He turned and lay down, a huddle in the dark. Jessa glanced at Hakon, who shrugged. They both hated this.

The night gathered, slowly. After the bitter journey Jessa found it hard to stay awake; without knowing she drifted into sleep. The others must have done so too, because a great snarling and roaring woke them all, in sudden terror.

She grabbed her knives and heaved the furs off. Moongarm's blanket was empty.

'The fool!' Brochael hissed.

He flung the door wide; Jessa stared under his arm.

The sky was black; ablaze with stars. The wolf and the bear, each glinting with frost, circled each other warily, the tethered goat bleating and squealing with terror.

The bear was huge, its pelt creamy-white, splashed with mud. It bared long teeth, snarling with hunger.

'Moongarm!' Kari's voice was sharp. 'Not yet!'

The wolf slavered at him, its eyes cunning. It crouched in the snow, its tongue hanging over wide jaws. Ignoring it, Kari came out of the house, Brochael close behind him.

Kari came forward over the snow. A little way from the bear he too crouched, still.

The bear did not move. Neither did the Snow-walker. None of the others heard their conversation.

For Kari the bear's mind was a white cave; a swirl of sharp scents, cold, the tang of blood. He reached in deeper, fascinated by the stream of instinct that drifted around him. In a place beyond words and speech, the bear's thoughts moved.

The bear was winter, it was white, it was huge. Wherever winter is, it said, there is terror, there is

158

cold. The cold comes from inside me. I am the ice; I am the vast frozen plains; they are all here, deep inside me, and yet I walk on them, cracking my thoughts with the weight of my wet fur.

I am winter, said the bear. How can you kill the cold, the frost, the wide, empty wind? I am all these. I am the stars, the aurora, the pain in your fingers and ears. I am the world's edge.

The bridge, Kari asked, struggling to keep his thoughts clear. What is the bridge? Is the bridge a rainbow?

But the bear answered no questions; its mind did not move that way. Its long chant began again, endless, as if its mind revolved on the same matter hour by hour. It snarled at him; Kari felt Brochael's anxiety; he dragged his mind out of the cold, reasonless hollows.

Standing up he said, 'It won't leave; it can't. Animals have no reason but their hungers. And this is a beast of myth. You'll have to do what you must.'

As he spoke, as if it had waited for this, the wolf leapt. Silent, it seized the bear's loose throat and dragged at it, snarling.

With a yell, Brochael ran out; Hakon behind him. Claws slashed; blood splattered the snow. The big man heaved his axe up and sliced at the bear's thick pelt; it roared in rage and tried to turn on him, but the wolf-jaws held it.

Then the bear shook the wolf off like a piece of rag; it turned and lumbered towards the men.

The wolf that was Moongarm staggered up, snarling, head low. Brochael, Hakon and Skapti stood, shoulder to shoulder. The bear paced towards them, growling.

'Ready,' Brochael muttered.

The wolf yelped; the bear swung, clumsily. The men yelled; they attacked together, defending each other, an axe and two swords, avoiding the fearsome claws and teeth, the great muscular limbs. In an uproar of fury the bear swung back; again the wolf leapt at its throat.

Hakon's sword slashed down.

The bear crumpled, dragging the wolf with it, striking at it, rolling on it, crushing it.

'It'll kill him!' Skapti gasped.

Breathless, Brochael gave a hiss of frustration and swung the axe high over his head. It caught the bear full in the neck; the beast shuddered; bones snapped under the blow.

It twitched and made a small, low rattle.

Then it lay still.

Silent, they all looked at it. Its fur lifted in the faint breeze. The wolf struggled out, gasping and wheezing; it stood, eyes blazing, blood dripping from its jaws.

It stepped towards them.

Brochael raised his axe.

For a long moment the tension hung. The wolf was battle-worn, savage; there was nothing human about it. Jessa felt her fingers clench; she wanted to shout, to warn Brochael to step back.

Then the wolf turned, as if with a great, silent effort. It loped into the smoke and mist.

'Moongarm!' Brochael snarled.

'I think,' the skraeling woman said quietly, 'it would be better to let him be. These shape-shifters carry the wildness in them for hours after a kill. They are not safe.'

'I'd be happy if we never saw him again,' Brochael muttered.

The skraeling looked down at the bear. 'This one and I have long been enemies.' Kneeling, she touched its muzzle. Perhaps she saw, as Kari did, the way its soul gathered on the snow; the white ghost-bear that wandered away into the frost. 'I honour you, bear,' she whispered. 'Your memory will not be lost.'

Later, she showed them the loom. It was dim, until the woman held the tallow-dip over it. Then they saw the cloth was coloured with brilliant dyes. There were battles woven in it, and voyages over blue seas, and great death struggles against the trolls of the dark. An old hero made the earth from an eggshell, made a kantele of pike-bones and sang the trees and clouds and mountains into being. And as Jessa looked closely the hanging moved before her, and she smelt the salt of the sea, and heard the leaves rustle. She saw herself and the others, and all their journey was there, all its fears and doubts, and now they were walking into the white, unwoven spaces. But the candle guttered, and she knew she had imagined that, and that none of them were there yet.

The woman turned to the poet. 'You will recognize this.'

He nodded, his sharp, lean face alight with pleasure. 'All poets weave this web, lady.'

They smiled at each other.

Moongarm did not come back. When they were ready to leave the travellers gathered, looking across the snow to the horizon.

'We can't wait for him,' Brochael said grimly. He

161

turned to the woman. 'I hope we haven't left you with a greater enemy.'

'We can't just go,' Jessa murmured.

'We can and we are.'

Skapti shouldered Moongarm's pack. 'I'll take this.'

'Leave it here.'

The skald shook his head. 'It's not heavy. He may catch us up.'

'I hope so,' Jessa said.

'I don't. We're well rid of him.'

'He may be hurt, Brochael!'

Brochael snorted. 'That one!'

The woman looked at him then. 'There are all sorts of pain, Brochael. Maybe there are some you do not recognize.'

He turned away.

They said goodbye, and the skraeling woman watched them go, the wind lifting the ends of her black hair. She folded her arms and called, 'If you come back, I'll be pleased.'

'We'll come back,' Jessa said.

The woman shook her head. 'You walk into the whiteness now. Into dreams. Only wraiths and sorcerers can live there.'

She turned and went back into the low house.

Jessa turned away. 'We never even asked her name,' she said.

21

On Hel's road all men tremble.

All day there was no sign of Moongarm.

The travellers walked through a perpetual twilight; for the first time the sun never rose above the horizon. Over them the icy stars swung in a great wheel, the polar star bright overhead. They walked on ice; immense tilted slabs of it, smashed here and there into jagged spars and shards that jutted up and had to be climbed and scrambled over.

A light snow fell on them; dusted them white with its touch. They saw nothing. No animals, no trace of anything alive in the long, pale-blue shadows of the ice-cap.

'He's staying behind,' Hakon joked. 'He's wise.'

After long hours they were frozen with cold; they ate the skraeling woman's food, and it put some heart back into them. Kari made a white rune-fire spark and crackle on the bare ice, but it had no warmth; there was nothing here to burn. They seemed to have lost all idea of time; the perpetual twilight confused them, as if time was something they were walking away from, leaving behind.

They tried to sleep there but the cold was too bitter.

'We'll carry on,' Brochael mumbled, scraping ice

from his beard. 'If we stay here we'll freeze. Come on.'

They staggered up and walked, almost uncaring. The wind rose, roaring from somewhere ahead over the empty miles and crashing against them. They were no longer a group; each one dwindled deep within himself, day-dreamed and imagined and sang silent songs. Speech died; their lips were too numb to shape words. At last, bone-weary, they dug a snow-hole and risked a short sleep there, out of the wind, but even that was dangerous. Blue and shivering, Jessa could hardly lift the food to her mouth.

Later, as they trudged on, she imagined that they were walking into the great white spaces at the top of the map; walking into blank parchment that no skald had ever written on, that held no words to make itself known.

Stumbling, ears throbbing, the skin under her scarves seared with the wind, she thought of Signi in that room, lying so still on the bed with its silken hangings. She felt those furs and blankets now; she was walking over them, up to Signi's mind, and they were warm, and all she had to do was lie down among them, like Signi, and sleep and sleep. But some nagging part of herself wouldn't let her; it ordered her, angrily, to shut up and keep walking.

Then Brochael murmured something, in awe.

Jessa stumbled; opened her eyes. Sleet stung her face like grit. And through her blurred eyes she saw, rising in a great arch against the dark sky, a bridge, glinting white. It was breathtaking; already it towered high above them, and she saw it glittered as if made of millions of crystals, fused to a solid mass.

Rainbows glinted deep within it; it shone against the snow-squalls.

The sight of it brought them back to themselves; they stood still, their breath ragged in the wind.

Then Skapti said, 'This will be my best song yet.'

'If you ever get to sing it,' Hakon muttered.

The skald wiped snow from his eyes. 'You're getting cynical, Hakon. Like me.'

They approached slowly, bent against the wind that tore at them. The ravens flew above, dim shapes against the stars, knocked sideways, squawking.

The ice here at the edge of the world was pitted with great cracks; they had to help each other over, scrambling and climbing, and all the time the scream of the wind increased; it raged in the terrible gap ahead of them, sending storms of snow and cloud churning high against the stars.

With an effort they gathered together, steadying each other. They had reached the foot of the bridge.

It was a fantastic, trembling structure; solid ice hanging in pinnacles and icicles of every thickness and length; frozen droplets bright as stars. The roadway itself was smooth as glass and looked slippery. On each side a delicate rail rose up, made of thin spines of ice spun in a fine paling, knotted with glassy balls.

Somewhere under the bridge, hidden in the falling snow, was the gap. The edge must be within feet of them, Jessa thought. Out of it there rose a howling and raging of wind; a stir of snow that twisted and burst.

The bridge rose into the storm and vanished. Of the other side they could see nothing.

'Right.' Brochael gathered them round him and

spoke loudly. 'I'll go first. Keep your heads down or the wind will blow you clean off. Hands and knees might be best.'

Skapti slapped him on the back, nodding.

Brochael put his hands to the slope and began to pull himself up. At each step he slid back a little, his boots scrabbling for toe-holds on the smooth glassy floor.

'It's possible,' he gasped. 'Barely.'

'Go on,' Skapti called. 'We're behind you.' He pulled Hakon over. 'You next, swordsman. Take your time.'

Hakon settled his swordhilt and smiled at Jessa.

'Be careful with your hand,' she said.

'I will. Good luck.'

He stepped up behind Brochael, bent low against the screaming wind. They both climbed slowly, gripping on anything they could. Under their feet the bridge was a glass hill, treacherous, beautiful. The others watched, the wind flapping their hoods and hair, until Brochael was a fair way up, the snowsqualls hiding him now and then.

Dragging his knees up under him he squirmed round and looked down at Hakon. 'Keep in the middle,' he roared. 'In the middle!'

But Hakon's foot had slipped; he slid sideways with a yell, sending a shower of crystals into the air, and began to slither, slowly, unstoppably, towards the frail ice uprights.

'Hakon!' Jessa screamed.

He scrabbled with his hands, with feet, with fingers, but nothing held; Brochael, scrambling down to him, cursed in the raging wind.

Hakon's foot met the ice pinnacles; for a moment

166

they held him, but as all his weight slid down on them they splintered; one snapped with a great crack, and with nightmare slowness he felt his legs sliding through the gap. Squirming, he grabbed at an icicle and heaved his sword out of the sheath, slamming it down flat on the wet surface. Then he drew himself up, and with all the strength of his terror he stabbed the blade down, hard, ramming it into the ice.

It held, and he clung on, the sword-grip so close to his face that the tiny red dragons blurred and moved in his wet eyes.

The wind tore at him. Below him was nothing; he hung over the edge of the world, swinging, clinging desperately to the sword that held him.

'Brochael!' he whispered.

'I'm coming. Hold on!'

Birds flew above him; the ravens. The glossy ends of feathers brushed his face, but they were wraiths, they couldn't help. No-one could. Numb, he knew he had been here before, long ago, in his dreams. He knew how it ended. And his hand, his weak right hand was aching to the bone, unclenching on the leather hilt, the fingers opening, loosening.

'Brochael!' he screamed.

Closing his eyes he felt the gale drag at him. Suddenly the sword slewed sideways; he yelled, grabbed at nothing, at a hand, a sleeve, warm fingers.

'Got you!'

Brochael's whisper was close; his face, huge, taut, the sweat freezing to crystals on his beard. He began to squirm back, and Hakon felt himself move; he was hauled up over the wet ice, swinging, until his knee came up and found the solid edge, and he heaved himself over and collapsed against Brochael, all breath knocked out of him.

For long seconds they lay there, dizzy, the sky glittering above them.

Only Jessa's desperate shouts stirred them.

Brochael waved. At this distance his words were lost, but the others saw he was safe.

'Thorsteeth!' Jessa breathed. She unclenched her gloves; felt the ache loosen between her shoulders. 'I thought they were gone.'

'So did I.' Skapti looked white. 'You next.'

She scrambled up, quickly.

'Keep your head down.'

She struggled up the glassy slope. It was very difficult. The wind forced against her; she crouched low, feeling for every treacherous, sliding step.

'Kari?' Skapti said.

But the boy had turned; he was looking back into the snow. Something moved in the squall; a great grey shape that leapt by him; with a snarl it had Skapti down and was standing over him, paws splayed, slavering at his throat with white teeth.

'Moongarm!' Jessa yelled. She stopped, looking back. Above her on the bridge Brochael roared with rage.

The wolf turned its head and looked at Kari, and there was something deep in those eyes that Kari knew, but it was lost, almost lost.

'All right,' Kari said. 'Let him up.'

The creature backed, snarling. Skapti scrambled to his feet, shaking.

'He wants me to go with him,' Kari yelled. He moved away, a small dark figure on the snow.

'You can't!'

168

'Go with the others. I'll be close behind.'

'Kari!' Brochael thundered.

Kari looked up at him; too far to hear, Brochael heard the words clearly, sharp with pain. 'Cross the bridge, Brochael. You must get them across the bridge.'

The squall blinded them for a moment; when they could see again the ice was empty.

'Kari!' Jessa yelled, furiously. 'Don't do this to us!'

But in all the miles of snow, there was no-one to answer her.

22

A third I see, that no sunlight reaches,
the doors face northward,
Through its smoke vent venom drips
serpent skins enskein that hall.

They crouched in a snow-hole, the blizzard lashing them. Shards of snow stung Kari's face; he tugged the scarves tighter.

The wolf had brought him here, leading him through the snow. Now it dissolved; became grey rags of mist that the wind whirled away. The man's body lay half buried; Kari scraped snow from the eyes and mouth, and lifted the head.

'Moongarm!'

He was cold, almost lost. Putting his thin fingers on the man's wrist, Kari searched desperately within him for the frail soul, dragging it to the surface. Ravens descended around him.

'He's gone,' one of them said harshly, crouching beside him.

'Not yet.'

The man gasped; his eyes flickered. Slowly the taints and wildness of the wolf were gathered into him; Kari felt them enter and flood the man. For a moment he had had the impression of someone gen-

170

tler, older; now it was gone, submerged. Moongarm's amber eyes watched him, intent. Snow roared between them.

'I have to get back,' Kari said. 'The others . . .'

'No!' He struggled up, his cracked fingernails gripping the boy's shoulder. Kari waited, uncertain. The man was still savage with the beast-nature that tormented him, but under that was fear, almost terror.

'Help me.' The words were quiet, nearly lost. 'Only you can.'

Kari shook his head. 'This power is your own.'

'I don't want it!' Moongarm snarled. 'It's taking me over – you can see that, you with your ghost-sight.' His face was grey, his hair streaked with ice. He crouched, head bent.

'When it began I could control it; I could change my shape and my nature as I wished. I was free, Kari! I could become something else, something wild, strong, fierce, without the troubles men have!'

'Without reason either.'

'Yes. But free.'

'You still can.'

'It's destroying me!' He paused, as if struggling for calm, his eyes wild and bright in his tangled hair. 'Every time, it takes me longer to come back. Gets harder. And even when I fight my way to man-shape the rage is still there. I'm changing. I think more and more like an animal thinks. Moods sway me, hungers, fears. I can't control them. After the bear died I was savage; those three men were just enemies, scents, I slavered for them. I didn't know their names, that they were Hakon, or Skapti, or even Brochael the stubborn. I have to get the wolf out of me, Kari. I have to!'

Kari wiped snow from his face. He was chilled to the bone; desperate to get back to the bridge. 'Why now?'

'The bridge. Once we cross it anything might happen.'

'To me,' Kari said bitterly. The rainbow shimmers of the ice-bridge came back to his mind.

'I need your sorcery. Reach in now and take the wolf out of me.' The man's eyes were close; his fingers closed tight as claws on the boy's arm. 'Now Kari! Before it devours me altogether. Before I run mad.'

Kari shivered, trying to think. Then he moved out of himself into Moongarm; walked down the track-ways of wolf-sight, saw the long loneliness of the man, the flung spears, barking dogs, the blood on the snow. He tasted endless arctic nights, the itch of fur, irrational terror. Then the wind splashed him with ice. He shook his head.

'I can't. Or if I did, it would kill you. It's too deep in you, Moongarm. You welcomed it in and it's tangled about you. Why?'

'A woman once offered me a chance of strength and courage. I was a weak man, of no family, no importance. Like a fool I took it.' Numb with cold and hopelessness he stared up at the ravens. 'Take it out, Kari.'

'No. One man is dead already because of me.'

Moongarm leapt up, sudden and supple. 'Then if you can't help, the gap will have me. The world's throat can take one more morsel.'

'No!' Kari jumped up quickly.

'You won't stop me, ravenmaster.'

'Won't I?' Kari gave him a cold, amused look. 'I

172

may seem frail Moongarm, but I can hold you to life. And I will!'

The wind blew his hair into his eyes; he shook it away. The shape-shifter stared at him through the scatter of snow.

'Then you will. And I must fight and struggle with myself. But if I can, Kari, I'll escape it, wherever I have to go. To have a power you dare not use is worse than having none.'

'I know that,' Kari said bitterly. 'Better than anyone.'

'Not much further!' Brochael yelled.

He was lost in the snow-squall ahead; Jessa couldn't see Hakon either. Behind her somewhere, Skapti slithered. She rested for a moment, crouched, her head low. Inside her frozen gloves her hands were blue and numb; her legs and back ached unbearably. She felt exhausted.

The bridge had been endless; first the climb high into nothing but sky and storm, and now the long scramble downwards, slipping and stumbling on the glassy slope. Briefly she thought of Kari and her anger and worry flared. Where was he? She was uneasy without him. Brochael must be too.

She looked up again; the bridge led away into blown snow, but through that she thought she could glimpse something else now, a shimmer of colours.

'Come on,' Skapti gasped behind her. He settled the bag with the kantele in it more firmly on his back. 'Not the time for dreaming, Jessa.'

'We're all hung about with dreams,' she said, scrambling up.

'Are we? Well this wind will blow them off. They'll

go sailing over the world's edge like spindrift.' A gust rocked him; he grabbed at her. 'Us with them, if you don't get on!'

She felt her way on, one hand on the frail ice-rail, the abyss roaring below. Her foot slid, testing the ice. Snow blinded her; she wiped it away, twice, and opened her eyes. The world was blurred. For a moment she stood still, in a sudden place of rainbows. Her hair and skin tingled; coloured lights moved all about her, they crackled, spat blue and green and purple sparks, glimmered, rippled over her face. She shivered with the eerie charge.

'What is it?'

'Surt's blaze. The aurora,' Skapti whispered. 'It's all around us.'

Blue and scarlet waves flowed over him; his clothes rippled gold and green. The crackle of colours enfolded them both, and under their feet the ice bridge broke the uncanny light and refracted it in a million tiny rainbows, deep within.

Not far ahead, someone called.

'That's Hakon.' Jessa scrambled forward, slid, fell on hands and knees.

Skapti hauled her up. 'Be careful!' he warned.

The bridge descended; they walked, blindly, into the coloured air, and wonderfully, after a few steps, they came out the other side, straight into a sudden cold stillness, the wind ending abruptly, as if an invisible wall of power held it back. The shock of that stillness, the relief of it, was enormous, and they both stopped, high in the sky.

Below them, they saw the land of the Snowwalkers.

Astonished, Jessa stared out at it. The sky here

174

was black, the stars brighter than she had ever seen them, a shining dust, flung to the horizon. Stretching from the foot of the bridge for miles and miles was an unbroken ice-sheet, smooth as marble, empty and featureless. Mountains rose in the distance; strange jagged peaks shining in the starlight, and among them, huge even from here, a building, a hall or fortress, tall and white and smooth behind a great encircling wall.

In silence they looked at it, across the miles of ice; at Gudrun's hall, in its silent, empty land, long-sought, long-feared.

At the foot of the bridge Hakon and Brochael were sitting, wearily.

Skapti said, 'So this is the land of dreams.' His voice was oddly choked; she looked at him sideways and he smiled, uneasily. 'Poet's visions, Jessa. Rarely do they come true.'

'Visions? Isn't this real?'

'I don't know any more. I think we left the world behind a long time ago. This is somewhere else; beyond the edge. The spirit realm.'

'I wish Kari was here,' she muttered.

When they got down to him, she knew Brochael was thinking the same. He gazed anxiously up at the rainbow bridge, arching into light. 'Where is he?'

'He'll come.'

'If he doesn't I'm going back. We can't do anything here without him.' He looked round, uneasily. 'Even the air smells of sorcery.'

It did. It was bitterly cold, and still, and had a strange tang of fear that Jessa found unnerving. Once or twice she thought she saw something move, out there on the ice, but the surface seemed empty, glimmering white.

Nothing would start a fire here, not even Brochael's tinderbox, and they were so tired that they lay down and slept as they were, in a dirty, windtangled huddle at the bridge's foot.

And it was then, in their sleep, that they knew the terror of the White People. Voices whispered around them, faintly. Cold fingers touched their hair and faces. The Snow-walkers came walking through their dreams, touching, laughing, mocking. They made Jessa dream of home, her farm by the sea, and in an instant she saw it dwindle to a black, charred ruin, open to the rain. She saw Signi, in thin chains of ice, calling her name. She saw Wulgar sitting alone in his hall, with a silvery woman at his shoulder, holding her hand out to him.

With a shiver of fear she opened her eyes.

They had been foolish to sleep; she knew that at once. Something had changed. Something was wrong. She stared around, dumbfounded.

A cage had been spun about them; fine spindly bars. They seemed easy to snap, but when Brochael struggled up and saw them he tried to wrench them apart with his huge strength. Nothing happened. He couldn't even grasp them. He swore, and looked at Skapti in alarm.

'It's no use,' the poet said quietly. 'Look out there.'

They turned, and saw.

Sitting watching them was an old, old man, his face wizened, his hooded eyes evil and bright. Coats and cloaks muffled him; the blue starlight played over his face.

He smiled at them.
Jessa recognized him at once.

23

Breath they had not, nor blood or senses,
Nor language possessed, nor life-hue.

'Grettir!' she breathed.

The old man smiled at them, a toothless grin.

'What have you done to us?' Brochael roared.

'What my people do, loud man. What my people do. I've caught you.' He scratched his head with a long hand. 'You haven't changed, girl. Still the fiery one. And here's Brochael Gunnarsson too, and the Wulfings' poet. All so far from home.'

Jessa sank down in despair.

'Who is he?' Hakon muttered.

'Grettir. Gudrun's counsellor. He was with her when she ruled in the Jarlshold – a sly creature, nearly as evil as she is. Did you never see him?'

He shook his head, staring at the pile of their weapons out there on the ice, the dragons on his sword hilt gleaming.

'I suppose,' Skapti said dryly, 'you don't intend a feast of welcome?'

'Clever.' Grettir coughed, a harsh, racking cough, and spat. 'No indeed. I've caught you in a cage of your own dreams. You can stay in there until you die – in this cold, very quickly. Then I might release you, and you can wander this land like all the other stolen souls. Unless of course . . .' He edged a little nearer, wheezing, 'Unless you tell me where the boy is.'

They were silent, glancing at each other. Jessa knew no-one would speak.

'I see.' The dwarvish man nodded. 'Misplaced loyalty, I'm afraid. Do you think I would harm him? His mother wants him alive.'

'We gathered that,' Skapti said.

Grettir nodded, grinning. 'Ah, I'd forgotten. Yes, we took the girl, if only to bring you here. If you knew that I find it strange that you should have come.'

'You would,' Jessa said scornfully.

'So then. Where is he? Why is he not with you?'

'He came before us,' Brochael said. 'He may be with Gudrun already.'

Grettir laughed slyly. 'Now that does not become you, my friend. I've been waiting here for you for many of what you call days, though here the stars are eternal. And no-one has come this way. I watched you come over the bridge, remember. I tasted your anxiety. He's not with you.'

'Maybe he's dead,' Skapti said, gravely.

Grettir looked at him. 'Maybe. In which case you can tell Gudrun, for I dare not. But I think that we'll wait and see. I know this, that he has her powers, and he'll feel the cold gripping you, the agony of your deaths. He'll know your danger. So we'll wait. In this land there is no hurry.'

They turned away from his smug grin, and squatted miserably on the frosty surface. Jessa felt so cold,

179

a bitter cold that seemed to pass right through her. The frost-cage held them firmly trapped.

'This is a nightmare,' she whispered.

Hakon nodded. 'And we're helpless.'

'If Kari comes,' Brochael muttered, looking up at the bridge, 'he'll walk straight into a trap. The old man must have something ready.'

'Kari might know.'

'And he might not. If only we could warn him! And Moongarm! What treachery has he brewed up?' He clutched his hands in frustration. 'If only I could get out!'

'Kari's grown, Brochael,' Skapti said. 'Grown in power. The old man might not have realized that.'

'It's too late anyway.' Hakon dropped his gaze from the bridge. Then he said, 'Take a look, but don't turn your heads. Don't let him know.'

Above the bridge, two tiny black flecks had soared out of the aurora light, becoming shadows among the starlight.

'The birds.' Jessa flicked a look at Grettir and saw with despair that the old man had noticed them too.

He chuckled and stood up, unsteadily. 'Ah. About time.'

'What are you going to do?'

He grinned at them. 'Let me give you a lesson. Do you know the time to steal a soul? The best, easiest time? As a man dies. It comes loose then, comes free. Almost anyone might reach out and take it – valkyrie, demon, sorcerer, Snow-walker. To take a soul from a living man takes great skill, enormous sorcery. Of all of us only Gudrun can do that. I can't. I must be content with a dead one.'

180

'You're going to kill him?' Jessa gripped the frost-rails. 'But you said . . .'

'I lied. His body will die. His wraith I will take to Gudrun. That's all of him she wants.'

His eyes lit; his long finger jabbed at the rainbow bridge.

'There!'

Two small figures had emerged from the nimbus of light; for a second they stood still up there, poised on the glassy arch. Jessa knew they were staring down at the empty land as she had done, feeling the relief of being out of the wind. Even from here she could recognize them; Kari's shining hair, pale in the moonlight, Moongarm just behind him, gripping the rail.

'Kari!' she screamed, leaping up. The others were shouting too, wild, useless warnings. For Grettir lifted his hand and spoke one word, a strange, ugly syllable.

And the bridge faded.

Like a rainbow fades, she thought, gripping her hands into hopeless fists. Through wet eyes she watched it go, lose substance, solidity; melt to a thing of light, through which the figures of her friends slipped, grabbed, fell, plunging down and down like small broken things into the mist. The storm of Ginnungagap swallowed them abruptly.

Their fall had been silent.

'Kari?' Brochael whispered.

Jessa turned away, sick and furious. Grettir was still, eyes closed, as if listening for something, reaching for it. She gripped the bars and wanted to scream at him, to kill him, and then she stopped, drawing a tight, painful breath.

From the pile of weapons Hakon's sword was

181

being lifted, lifted by an invisible hand. It came floating through the air to the back of Grettir's neck and jabbed.

The old man stiffened, eyes wide. Astonishment and dismay passed over his face. Then he nodded, appreciatively. 'Clever,' he murmured.

Jessa grabbed Brochael's arm and forced him round. 'Look!' she gasped, warm with joy. 'It's all right! They're alive!'

Slowly Moongarm became visible to them all. He held the sword point against the old man's neck. 'Sit down,' he snarled, 'and do nothing, sorcerer. I wouldn't like to soil my friend's sword.'

The old man crumpled. He seemed ruefully amused. 'She said you were unpredictable, Kari. I had not guessed how much.'

'Hadn't you?' Kari stood on the ice, the ravens flapping out of nothing about him. 'Are you sure about that?'

Grettir looked up at him, and his face changed. After a moment he said, gravely. 'You have grown so much like her.'

Kari said nothing to that. He came over to the cage and gripped the bars.

'Can you do it?' Skapti asked.

'I think so.'

Hakon shook his head. 'We saw you fall!'

'I'm sorry.' Kari looked at Brochael. 'I had to make it look like that. We'd crossed earlier. I had a warning. Long ago.'

Brochael nodded, numb with cold. He reached out and touched Kari's sleeve. 'I should have known,' he said, his voice gruff. 'Get us out of here.'

The bars dissolved; they melted to nothing. And all the world went with them, into darkness and cold.

Someone was chafing her fingers and hands; numbly she felt the pain throb back into them, the hot pulse of blood.

She opened her eyes, slowly. Brochael's bulk loomed against mist and starlight. He said, 'You're all right. You're back.'

She was wrapped in blankets, chilled to the bone. A fire was burning on the ice, crackling and sparking; for a moment she wondered how, and then realized Kari must have made it; a rune-fire, but giving out wonderful heat. Then she saw the sack burning in it, and the thin, familiar spars of wood. It took her a long moment to realize what they were.

Appalled, she sat up.

Skapti brought her a cup of warm water and some salt fish. She took it, staring at him. 'How could you?' she asked gently.

'No choice. We had to get warm.' He smiled wanly towards the burning wood of the kantele. 'There'll be plenty more songs, Jessa, if we get out of this, don't worry. They're in me. She won't undo them. Not the trees in my forest.'

She nodded, sadly, wondering what he meant. Her body felt strange; cold at the edges, like a house no-one has lived in for a while. She flexed her toes and fingers, her shoulders.

Grettir was sitting quietly by the fire, Moongarm close beside him. They were taking no chances, but the old man seemed content just to sit, as if he accepted his plan had failed. But his bright eyes

183

gleamed at Jessa under his hood, and she knew he was laughing at them all.

She must have been asleep a long time; the stars had moved round in their great silent wheel. Otherwise everything looked the same. The land glimmered, pale and empty.

Kari was talking. 'Half way over I knew something was wrong, but not what. We had to come unseen.'

Skapti shook his head. 'It's cost me a year off my life.'

Brochael said nothing; he put his big arm round Kari and squeezed him.

'And now what?' Hakon asked.

'Now we go to Gudrun.' Kari said firmly. 'Alive.'

Grettir shook his head and smiled slyly. 'For now, little prince. For now.'

24

The planets knew not what their places were.

They walked through an empty land, without time. It was a country where nothing grew, where even the wind dared not come. Soft snow fell silently through the long, arctic night; it was a realm of starlight and sorcery, beyond the world. Since they had entered it, each of them had felt a constant fear, a strange diminishing of themselves. They were no longer sure who they were or how real this was – in this place anything could happen. Even the air was alive, tingling with power.

They walked together, in a group; only Kari walked a little way in front, the birds above him. He said nothing, but all his old apprehension seemed to have fallen from him; he had put on that coat of power, that air of remoteness they knew. He was ready now, Jessa thought. And for whose death? Because only he or Gudrun would survive. Once they had walked away from each other. But not now. This would be the end.

The fortress loomed nearer, a hall built from icy blocks, fitted together with sorcerous skill. The gates were open; they were entanglements of ice, sharp shards of bright crystal. Grettir walked in between them, limping; the travellers followed him with drawn swords.

A great courtyard stretched before them; they crossed it quickly, watching the high windows. Hakon glanced back. Only their footprints marred the smooth snow. And yet they all knew they were being watched.

Only Kari saw them, as he passed by; the great host of the Snow-walkers, talking, laughing, amused, curious. They were a pale people, their faces as thin and delicate as his own. Children among the crowd stared at him; men and women with white snake-marks in their skin. Gudrun's people. His people. It moved him; apart from Gudrun he had never seen anyone who looked as he did. Turning away, bitterly, he faced the doors.

They were open.

Grettir stopped on the bottom step. When he got his breath he wheezed, 'From here you go in by yourselves.'

'While you lock the doors?' Brochael grabbed the old man's arm, roughly. 'Oh no. Show us where Signi is.'

Grettir shrugged. 'It makes no difference, in the end.'

'It might to you, if you want to live. Where is she?'

'Through the hall. Up the stairs.'

The hall was bitterly cold, a palace of ice. It was bare of furniture; snow lay in tiny waves on the floor, crunching as they walked over it, but its splendour was in the light that came through the ice; a pale shimmer of blue and green, a refraction of stars and snow, eerie and cold. On some of the walls were hangings, all white and silver, and shields of strange metals. Ice girders held up the roof; thin spindles of ice hung from each windowsill, and great curtains of it, formed over years, massed here and there, sprawling out into the floor to make pillars and columns of intricate crystal. It was a frozen house, without sound, or welcome.

On the far side of the hall were some stairs, leading up.

'These?' Brochael snapped.

Grettir nodded.

Kari leapt up the first steps lightly; the others clattered after him.

'Where are they all?' Hakon breathed to Jessa. 'We're walking into a trap, I'm certain.'

'I know that. We all do. Stick behind me if you're scared.'

He smiled, but it was a wan effort.

The ice-steps led up between glinting walls. Then they came out into a room at the top. Crowding into the doorway behind Hakon, Jessa caught her breath.

The room was a blaze of candles; white candles of every size and thickness. The flames burned straight, with no breeze to flutter them. In the centre of the room was a white chair, and Signi was sitting in it, staring at them. She held out her hands.

'I almost hoped you wouldn't come,' she said, sadly.

'We had to.' Skapti crossed to her.

'Is Wulfgar . . .?'

'He's not with us. He had to stay at the hold.'

Her dress and hair seemed paler here, drained of colour; her skin had a strange, glistening tinge. The back of the chair was a network of ice strands, hung and looped, great chains of it. They dropped from her sleeves and wrists, unwound and slithered after her as she stood up and crossed the room.

She tried to touch them, but her fingers passed through Brochael's and he shook his head.

'How do you like your sword, Hakon?' she asked.

Puzzled, he glanced down at it. 'Very much, but the gift was a long time ago.'

'Was it?' She looked at them carefully, at their worn clothing, and windburned, unshaven faces. Fear crept into her eyes. 'How long?'

'Weeks.'

She pressed her fingers together, pale and trembling. 'I didn't know. There's no time in this place. Nothing but silence and cold, no-one to speak to or touch . . . Her eyes darted to the doorway, where Grettir stood. He smirked at her.

Kari fingered the chains, thoughtfully.

'Can you?' Jessa asked him.

'No. This is Gudrun's spell. Only she can.'

'You should leave here!' Signi put her wraith-hand on his; only he could feel her, frail as a leaf. 'You shouldn't have come, Kari. It's you she wants! She only brought me here to bring you.'

'I know that.' He turned to Grettir, reluctantly. 'Where is she?'

'Waiting for you.'

'Then show me where. But I want to know that nothing will happen to my friends. Either way. I want to be sure of that.'

'Oh no!' Jessa said firmly. She caught his arm, tight. 'You're not vanishing on me again! We're all in this.'

He tried to tug away, but she had been expecting this; she held tight.

'Jessa . . .'

'No, Kari.'

Grettir watched them, amused. 'Touching,' he murmured.

'Keep out of this,' Brochael growled. He put his hand on Kari's shoulder. 'She's right.'

Kari glared at them both. 'I don't want to hurt you . . .'

'Nor will you.'

'. . . But you have to let me go! Please Brochael!' He squirmed away from them.

'Not without us.' Brochael caught him again, firmly. 'Listen Kari, Jessa is right. We're all in this, it isn't just you. You can't take it all on yourself.'

'And what good do you think you will be to him?' a cold voice mocked. 'The boy is no kin of yours, Brochael Gunnarsson. He's nothing of yours. He's mine. And always will be.'

Brochael stood still. His face hardened, and as he turned he put his arm round Kari and they stood together, looking at the woman in the doorway.

25

*His hands he washed not nor his hair
    combed.*

She looked older.

She was tall still though, and pale; her long hair braided and caught in a shining net. Her coat was the colour of snow-shadows, blue and dim in the strange ice-light, her eyes colourless and impossible to read.

She stepped quickly into the candlelight, her silks and furs swishing, and she smiled at them, that cold, indifferent smile that had terrified Jessa so long ago.

Glancing at Kari she said, 'You only have to look at us.'

They all watched her, uneasy. Gudrun had worked her spell on each of them, Jessa thought. She had once made Hakon a thrall, crippled in one hand, useless but for slow, endless labour. She'd sent Jessa herself into the terror of Thrasirshall, stolen Wulfgar's kingdom, made Skapti an outlaw scavenging for years on favours and carrion. Brochael she had banished to die with her son, and from him, Kari, she had taken everything, left him unable to speak, walk, even to think, not knowing what people were.

190

His very father had never seen him. And then she'd murdered his father.

Each of them had deep cause to hate her. Only Moongarm stood aside.

Gudrun crossed the room and put her hands out to Kari. 'I knew you would come home.'

'This isn't my home.' He stepped back.

'Yes it is,' she said, seriously. 'You've seen that, seen the people here. My people and yours. I heard you think it, Kari. You can't deny that.'

He turned away, then back to face her, abruptly. 'You've offered me this before. I don't want it.'

She nodded, and smoothed her dress in the old gesture that Jessa remembered. 'Then let me show you something that you do want. All of you. What happened in the Jarlshold was my spell, yes, but the dreams that destroyed you were your own. Dreams of mortals. Destructive, dangerous. Look here, and see what you do to yourselves.'

In the middle of the room she opened her hands, almost carelessly, and spread a coldness about her, a darkness in the air that surrounded them all swiftly. The room faded; they seemed to be standing in snow, knee-deep in it, somewhere outside.

Jessa looked around fearfully. It was the Jarlshold, she knew. But how it had changed!

The silence was deathly. Thick snow coated everything; icicles hung over shutters and sills. Between the riven clouds a few stars glimmered, and showed her that the snow was unmarked. The settlement seemed totally deserted.

Gudrun lifted the doorlatch; the familiar door to the Hall. It opened, slowly.

'It was cunning of you to leave a guardian,' she

said, glancing at Kari. 'Otherwise I should have had them all by now.'

They stepped warily into the hall.

It was frozen, stiff with ice. Gloom hung in its spaces, a silence of sleep. Walking in the vision over the stone floor, Jessa saw sleeping forms all around her, huddled up, barely breathing in the searing cold. They were all here now; the fishermen, farmers, children, thralls, the women and the warband, some crumpled where they had fallen, others covered with blankets or furs.

Ahead of her, deep in the gloom, a glint of red light showed, smouldering, barely alive. Someone was still awake.

As they came closer Jessa saw it was the embers of a fire, the dull peats giving out a faint heat. Over it one man was huddled, wrapped in a dark blanket, and as he raised his head and looked at them she saw it was Wulfgar.

His appearance shocked her. He was thin, almost gaunt. A dark stubble covered his chin and his red-rimmed eyes looked weary and unfocused. He smiled bitterly when he saw them. 'Now I know I'm delirious. Are you dead then, all of you? Are you ghosts, come to haunt me?'

'A vision,' Kari said, crouching by him. 'Nothing more.'

Wulfgar did not seem to hear him. He shook his head and gave a low, bitter laugh. 'Of course you are. Dead at the world's end, where I sent you. And all of us here caught in her spell, except me. Gods, I wish I was too.'

He clasped his hands round his sword-hilt and turned away from them, staring into the flames.

Skapti stood rigid, watching him. Then he turned on Gudrun. 'I could kill you myself for this.'

She smiled coldly at him.

'He can barely see us,' Kari murmured. 'He thinks he's imagining us.'

'But why is he still awake?' Jessa asked.

Kari crossed to the roof-tree; the great ash-trunk rose above him, glinting with frost. 'Because of this.'

They gathered round him and saw, wedged into a deep cleft at the base of the tree, something that shone in the firelight. Jessa moved back to let the light through and suddenly they saw what it was; a small piece of crystal, covered with spirals. For a moment she wondered where she had seen it before, and then the memory came to her of Kari's strange tower room in Thrasirshall. The crystals had hung there in long strings from the roof. She remembered them turning in the sun.

'This protects him?' Brochael asked.

'Yes.' Kari turned defiantly to the witch, who stood a little back. 'You'll never get it out. I made sure of that.'

The vision of the hall vanished instantly; they were in the candlelit room, and Signi was crying, quietly, into her hands.

'That doesn't matter,' Gudrun said easily. 'None of that matters now. I wanted you to come and you have.'

She touched his sleeve, teasing. 'This is where you belong. Stay here, and I'll release them, all of them. These can go; the Jarlshold will be free. I have no interest in them.'

'Kari, no.' Brochael warned.

The boy was silent.

'And think about this,' Gudrun went on, quietly. 'Here, you are one of us. No-one will point you out because you're different, or stiffen in terror if you look at them. I always enjoyed that, but I think it pains you. Among them you'll always be an outsider, and that will never change Kari, never, no matter how much they think they know you. Can you live with that all your life?'

For a moment they stood together, two identical faces, Gudrun's watchful, Kari's downcast. Then he pulled his arm away from her.

'Leave me alone!' he said bitterly. 'You've done this to me before! I won't let it happen again. We've come too far, been through too much. These are my friends; I trust them. They trust me.' He gripped his hands together and went on, rapidly. 'And I need them. I need them to keep me from becoming like you. I care about them, and about Wulfgar, and all the people you've stolen from themselves. I can't turn my back on them. Not now.'

'Well said,' Brochael growled.

'Can you understand that?' Kari went close to her, almost pleading. He was as tall as she was now, Jessa noticed with surprise. Face to face he confronted her, snatching her thin hands. 'Can you?' he breathed.

Gudrun smiled at him, almost sadly. 'No,' she said. 'And you know that means death for one of us.'

Her words were like a blow.

Brochael stepped closer but she looked through him, unconcerned. 'I've never known you, Kari,' she said. 'You and I have always been on opposite sides of the mirror.'

'We don't have to be,' he whispered.

'I see now that we do. It's too late, my son. Too late for everything.'

And they were gone, instantly, both of them.

Jessa gasped with shock and rage; Brochael swore in fury. 'Where are they?' he roared, swinging round.

But the old man had gone too.

26

What do you ask of me? Why tempt me?

Kari was standing in darkness.

Around him were many invisible people; he could feel their thoughts crowding him and he pushed them away. He knew this was the spirit-world, the dream-realm. Anything could happen here, so he made some light; it flooded the room.

He was in a small place, little more than a cell. A dirty bed lay on the floor in one corner, and on the hearth the ashes were cold. A tiny window let in starlight, over his head.

He knew where this was. The memory came over him, sharp and bitter, and then it was a weariness, a familiar relentless numbness that crept over his mind.

He went across and knelt on the grey blankets, fingering the scrawls on the wall, the marks made with a charred stick, all blurs and spirals.

'Why here?' he murmured.

'Because of all the places in the world this is the one you fear most.' She leaned against the damp wall looking down at him, as she always had. 'They don't know, your friends, about this terror, do they? About the nightmares of this room? Not even Brochael?'

Kari sat on the worn blankets, knees up, hugging

himself. He rocked back and forth a little, saying nothing.

'How empty they were,' she said softly, coming to stand over him. 'All those years in here.'

'You locked me in here. Abandoned me . . .'

'Years of silence. Fear. You remember them?'

'I can't forget.' He looked up, fiercely. 'Why did you do that? It could all have been so different. For both of us.'

She shook her sleek head, kneeling before him, her silk dress rustling in the straw. 'Among us, there can be only one soul-thief. I knew that from the beginning.'

Kari barely heard her. He was fighting to stay calm, to beat off the terrors of his childhood. All around him he felt them coming out, from the walls, from the blown ashes, from the marks he had drawn years ago, a child without thoughts, frightened and cold, unable to speak.

He knew every inch of this place, had fingered every crack of it, crawled in every corner, watched the slow forming of frosts every winter, the moving wand of sunlight that stroked out the dreary days. Now it seemed as if he had never left. All that had happened since grew faint and unreal; he knew this place was the emptiness in him, the yearning, the source of all her power over him. As he crouched there he began to forget them all, Jessa, Skapti, even Brochael; speech began to die in him, so that he groped for words and had forgotten them, even their sounds. There was only the woman, the tall woman, and he could never escape from her, never. He had been here too long.

Far outside him, something flapped and squawked;

197

he looked up with a great effort and saw a raven's beak prising at the window bars.

Gudrun smiled. 'Even those I can keep out.'

Miserably, he put his hands out to her, and she took them. And with a strength and suddenness that astonished him he felt her reach into him, deep among his thoughts and terrors and memories, until she touched, with a cold finger, his soul. And she began to tug at it, and he felt his personality quiver and fail, and as he slumped away from her against the stone wall he knew numbly that she was drawing out his very being, dragging it from him, and he crumpled to his knees, clutching the grey blanket with a child's thin fists.

'Stay with Signi,' Brochael ordered.

Moongarm stared at him. 'I'm surprised you trust me.'

'So am I,' Brochael snarled. 'Keep the door shut.'

He slammed it from the outside himself, the others behind him.

'They could be anywhere,' Skapti muttered.

'Not even visible.'

'I don't care, Jessa!' Brochael was aflame with wrath. 'We'll tear this place to pieces till we find someone, somewhere! She won't take him away from me. Never!'

He raced down the stairs; the others followed, reckless.

The ice hall was bare and silent; the rooms on each side of it deserted. Skapti flung their doors wide, one after another.

'Nothing!'

'She's here!' Rubbing frost from his face, Brochael

stopped. He slammed a fist into the wall. 'She's got to be.'

'She'd have a room,' Jessa said thoughtfully.

'What?'

'A room. A place of her own . . .'

'For her sorceries, yes, I know! But where?'

'High up, like Kari's.' Jessa turned decisively. 'There must be other stairs. Split up, quickly. Try every room.'

She ran into the nearest narrow entrance; it led her to a small store-room piled with chests of strange white metal. Putting the point of her knife under the lid of one she forced it open. A sudden yellow glow lit her face; she gazed down at huge lumps of amber, gloriously coloured. A treasure beyond price. And the other chests would hold jet and ivory and silver, all Gudrun's hoard.

But there was no time for it now. She slammed the lid down and ran back out. Skapti thumped into her. 'Anything?'

'No. What about . . .'

Hakon's yell silenced her; it was distant, far across the hall. When they got to him he was leaning against a wall of frost, breathless.

'There,' he managed.

The doorway was small, hung with icicles. Beyond it steps descended, down into darkness. A cold, sweet smell hung in the air.

'Down?' Jessa muttered.

'She's his opposite, remember?' Hefting the axe in his great hands, Brochael led the way, grimly.

The stairs ran deep into the ice. As they clattered down it the air grew colder, bitterly cold, their breath a glinting fog. Light faded to blue-green gloom. They knew they were far down in the ice-layers, deep inside the glacier. On each side of them the walls became opaque, then mistily transparent; far inside them bubbles of air were trapped, like soft crystal shimmers.

Brochael stopped, abruptly. 'We were right.'

The doorway at the bottom was a small one, but carved deep in the ice above it was a great white serpent. It curled around the lintel, its sightless eyes glaring down at them. From within came sounds; a murmur of voices.

'They're in there,' Hakon muttered.

Brochael gripped the axe. His face was set. 'Ready?'

'Ready.'

'Brochael!' Jessa's scream of warning was just in time; he turned, and in the corner of his eye saw the movement flash; then the snake struck at where his head had been, its venom sizzling the ice.

'Gods!' He jerked back, shoving Hakon aside.

The snake hissed; a thin tongue flickered from its ice-lips. Then quickly it unwound itself from the doorway, slithering down the pillars towards them.

Hakon was closest; he struck at it in disgust, and the sword sliced deep into the cold, impossible flesh. But it came on, slipping round his blade, his wrist and arm, and he yelled and squirmed in terror.

'Keep still!' Brochael roared.

He and Skapti tore at the wet, slippery body; it hissed and spat at them, darting at their eyes, tightening its muscles round Hakon with a fierce gripping pain that made him cry out. Jessa slid behind Brochael, knives in hand. The pale scaly back rippled

200

before her. Choosing her time, she pulled her arm back and thrust, deep and hard.

Like a distant shock, Kari felt the stab.

For a moment his mind cleared; he reached out and pushed her away, knotting darkness and runes to a wild web of protection that she tore to fragments in seconds. Fierce and hungry she dragged at him, and he struggled to fight her off, to stand. Outside, something thumped and thudded. From an immense distance a voice yelled 'Kari!' – a voice he knew, a voice that stirred him. And he remembered. He remembered the day when the door had opened and the stranger had come. A man such as he had never seen, huge and red and bearded, a lantern gleaming in his hand. And he knew that the man's name was Brochael, and grasping that he felt his life flood back to him, his thoughts and speech, the faces of his friends. Power surged in him; he stood up, shakily.

Gudrun grabbed his hands again, her nails cutting deep.

'Stay with me,' she hissed.

Numb, he shook his head. Then, summoning all his sorcery, he tore her spell apart.

The walls soared upwards, the window rippled, became a wide casement of glass, open to the sunlight. With a cry he let the cell split open; it became a tower room hung with long strings of threaded crystals that twirled and glittered in the cold, brilliant light. With a shrill kark of triumph the ravens broke through; they flapped through the window and perched, one on a table, the other on the rim of a bowl.

Kari sat down, in his usual chair. He was weak with the effort it had cost him.

And Gudrun gazed around at it all, furious.

27

The children of darkness, the doombringers.

'Perhaps this is the place you fear most,' he said quietly. He felt drained already; weary from the desperate struggle to hold onto himself. Now he reached out and touched the hangings of quartz, setting them swinging. The bird-wraiths stood behind him; he knew she saw them as he did; two tall men. One laid a narrow hand on his shoulder.

'Where is this?' she demanded, her voice clotted with wrath.

'You know where, though you've never been here. This is Thrasirshall. The place you sent me to die.' Shaking his head he smiled, wanly. 'The strange thing is it was here I learned how to live.'

Gudrun looked coldly around her, at the sparse room, at the bird-wraiths. 'I see. And now you think you're a match for me?' She laughed at him, her eyes bright, and he felt his heart sink, as it always did before her.

'My powers are too much for you, Kari. I've had years of practice. Try if you like but remember this. Of all our people, only I can steal souls.'

He looked up at her, and knew his danger.

'Until now,' he said.

Moongarm looked sidelong at Signi. 'What does it feel like?' he murmured.

She shook her head, the pale hair swinging. 'As if I'm adrift. Nowhere.'

He crossed the room and picked up the ice-chain. 'That's a feeling I know about.' He ran it through his hands, over the sharp, broken nails.

'So why did you come with them?' she asked quietly. 'Why here?'

'You've guessed why.' He flung the chain down and turned away from her, a lean uneasy figure in the white room. 'Because the spell that's on me came from here. I didn't know that at first, didn't know who the woman was. I never saw her again. But as I wandered north, an outcast, hated, chased away from every settlement, I heard the tales of them, the sorcerers at the world's end, a pale, dangerous people. I thought then she must have been one of them. When I saw the boy I knew. But he can't help me. And then, just now, there she was, standing in that doorway. The same woman.'

'Gudrun?'

'It was years ago, but I knew her. She looked at me, but I saw that she's forgotten me. Forgotten.'

'She's hurt us all . . .'

'But I asked her for this. I asked her! And I was glad of it. At first I thought she had made me more than a man. Not less.'

He brooded bitterly, watching the floor with his strange amber eyes. She felt sorry for him, and suddenly afraid.

'Moongarm . . .'

He crossed to the door. 'I have to go. You'll be safe enough.'

'Moongarm wait!' She stood up, the ice-chain tinkling. 'Leave it to Kari!'

Sword in hand he looked back at her and shook his head. Then he opened the door and slid out.

Painfully Jessa picked herself up off the floor, where the thrashing of the snake had flung her. Hakon lay on his stomach, coughing for breath; he rolled over and stared at her.

A long wet stain scored the ice between them; it froze as they watched, into a stinking shimmer of crystal. The knife too, was coated with ice; she wiped it in disgust against the side of her boot.

'All right?' Brochael asked.

Hakon nodded, getting up. 'Was it alive?'

'As alive as I wanted,' Skapti said. 'I could even have done with a little less.'

'Don't waste time!' Jessa snapped.

'She's right.' Brochael turned to the door. 'Open it.'

She lifted the latch and pushed, suddenly. The door swung wide without a sound, but despite their hurry none of them made any move to enter. Because what lay beyond the door was not a room, or a place in any world they knew. It was a nothingness, a mist of light, and figures loomed and moved in it, receding into distances that were too far. They knew this was the spirit-realm, the place where Kari sometimes went, in the darkness, under the stars. But if they were to go in, how could they ever get back, Jessa thought.

She glanced at Skapti. 'Do we?'

'No!'

Brochael turned. 'We have to! Kari is in there.'

'And Kari knows far more about it than we do.'
The skald crossed to him, took his arm with long,
firm fingers. 'I know it's hard Brochael, but we can't
just blunder in. We might not be helping him. We'd
be putting ourselves in danger.'

'He's right,' a sly voice muttered.

Grettir stood behind them on the stairs, a tiny,
hunched figure in his coats and wraps. He rasped out
a chuckle. 'Go in there and you'll wander for ever.'

'You would say that!' Brochael came back and
caught the old man by the throat, all his frustration
infuriating him. 'Tell me the truth now, before I
squeeze the life out of you. What's happening to
them?'

Grettir still smiled. 'A contest of souls, axeman.
And only one of them will come out of it alive.'

He reached out at her, through sunlight and mist.
Through unbearable coldness into empty places, into
nothing. With all his power he reached for her soul
– and touched ice. He took out his knife and began
to dig at it, chipping and stabbing, kneeling on a
glacier, out in the cold. Somewhere, she was laughing
at him; he ignored that. A little way off, dark against
the stars, all the Snow-walkers watched.

It was hard, tiring work; fiercely he chipped at the
ice and shards of it flew up in his face; he jerked
back, afraid for his eyes. Hands pulled at him, voices
murmured, but he shrugged them off.

'Keep them away!'

The bird-wraiths moved behind him, menacing.

And now deep in the glacier something gleamed;
he pushed his fingers in among the crushed slush and
tugged it out; a stone, a diamond, hard and glittering.

It burned him and he almost dropped it. It became a snake winding over his fingers, a bird fluttering in his hands, a flame, a drift of vapour, a stinging wasp, but still he held it, through all the pain and the woman's growing anger, all around him.

'Even though you've found me,' she hissed. 'You won't keep me.'

'I will. This time.'

She was there, feeling for his hands, opening his fingers, but he flung her off and held on.

She came again, her hands soft on his. 'I'm your mother,' she said, 'Remember?'

'I know that.' Despite himself, tears blinded him; he held the stone fiercely, huddled over it. 'But that's over. All of it. Everything is over.'

Then she knew. With a scream of rage and fear she struck at him; became a coldness that closed about him tight, tearing at his life, but he held the diamond tight. And it was her soul that he held, and her power and anger and amazement, and he let it flow into himself, feeling that he knew her for the first time, knew all of her, and it terrified him.

'Let me go!' her voice screamed. 'Let me go!'

Dragging all his energies about him, Kari began the webs; he conjured with runes and blackness and cold, pulled out every shred of power he had to wind about her, to hold her, to keep her still. Murderous with rage she tore at him, became a flame that burned him, lava that seared his hands but he knew he was holding on, that he was winning, and the power in him grew and he wound the spells tighter, fiercer, binding them about her.

Somewhere, someone was shouting, but he couldn't think about that now, he had to imprison

207

her; his hand slid to his pocket and he pulled out the crystal he had brought for this.

Deep within it he embedded Gudrun's soul, deep in the sharp glass facets, weaving spells about her with words that came from nowhere into his mind, as if all the sorcery of the Snow-walkers rose up and flooded him now. And when the spell was finished, when he was sure it was safe, he closed his eyes and let his mind empty, and there was silence, and exhaustion swept over him like a wave.

'Is it done?' a harsh voice croaked in his ear.

Numb, he nodded.

'Then you must get back. This is nowhere. We're lost here. Now, runemaster!'

'Later,' he murmured.

'Now! It must be now, Kari!'

They crowded him close, anxiously. All he wanted to do was sleep, to lie down and rest, but he knew they were right, and he staggered up, his hand gripping the crystal.

'Which way?'

'Any way! It's all one.'

Nodding, struggling to think, he stumbled forward into the dark, into a mist that swirled purple and green and then white, ice-white.

And as the others stood at the door they saw him drift towards them, loom suddenly out of nowhere, and Jessa swore that for a moment two men were with him, until the mist swirled and she saw they were only the ravens, swooping out, eyes bright.

But Kari was indistinct; he stumbled as he came, and just as he reached the threshold he almost fell. Brochael caught him, but at the same time Moongarm pushed from behind and snatched something out of Kari's hand, snatched it fiercely, hungrily, a small, glittering stone.

'No!' Kari gasped.

Brochael grabbed the man's sleeve.

'Let me finish this,' Moongarm said, quietly.

'No!' Kari struggled to stop him. 'Brochael!'

'You know it's best,' the were-man said. 'I'll take this where no-one will ever find it. Where she'll never get back. Call it my revenge. And it's what you want, Brochael.'

Slowly, Brochael let go of his sleeve. Then he said, gruffly. 'It's taken me too much time to come to know you.'

'And now you do?'

'I think so.'

Moongarm nodded at him. 'I'm glad, my friend.'

And then he turned and walked through the door-way, deep into the mist, and as he walked his body twisted and blurred to a lithe, grey creature, shimmering, gone in an instant.

Kari turned away, silent.

And over his shoulder the others saw nothing but a small frozen room, every surface of it seamed with ice, and in a white chair Gudrun was sleeping, just as Signi had slept.

28

Unsown acres shall harvests bear,
Evil be abolished.

Kari slept for a day and a night, almost without moving. The others stayed alert. They gathered in Signi's room, not knowing what to expect, and Brochael prowled about uneasily, axe in hand. But no-one came near them. The ice-fortress stayed as it had always been, cold and silent.

Finally, Jessa and Hakon ventured out. Food was running short, and they needed to find out what the Snow-walkers were doing.

Creeping silently into the hall they saw a strange sight. Grettir was huddled in a small chair, his palms flat on the carved armrests. On a white bier before him Gudrun lay asleep; she lay still, barely breathing, her long hair loose, her dress smooth and white. Icicles already hung from her sleeves; crystals of frost had begun to form on her hair and skin.

They walked up to her, and looked down, in awe.

'She looks as though she'll wake up at any moment,' Hakon whispered.

'She won't.' Jessa looked down at the old man. 'What happens to you?'

Grettir stirred and looked up. His face was lined and grey. 'That depends. Does the boy live?'

'Yes.'

'Then we're all in his hands. He has the power now.'

He stood up and shuffled towards the sleeping woman, and looked down at her, thoughtfully. 'She was cruel too often, but she was strong. She knew all the secrets, she took what she wanted. Until the end, she was never afraid.'

He glanced at Jessa who said, 'She was evil. We all knew that.'

'And now Kari comes into his inheritance. How different will that be?'

'Very different,' she snapped.

He laughed, wheezily. 'I'm glad you think so. But I know better. I know how their power gnaws them till they must use it; how it changes them. Even she was different once.'

'But Kari's got something she never had.'

'What?'

She smiled at him. 'He has us.'

For a moment he looked at her gravely, and at Hakon, and then he smiled too. 'So he does,' he said, sadly. 'I hope that it will be enough.'

He turned, and hobbled away. 'I'll bring you some food.'

'Thank you.'

'We didn't even ask him,' Hakon murmured.

'That's how this place is.'

'And it's Kari's now. Will he stay here?'

'I don't know.' Thoughtfully, she walked to the door.

211

Grettir brought the food; strange stuff, most of it, but they ate it and saved some for Kari. When he finally woke up he sat by Brochael for a while, listless and silent, no-one wanting to bother him with questions. Finally, with an effort, he got up and went over to Signi.

'You must go home now,' he said.

The girl smiled at him, her silken dress pale. He touched her wrists briefly and the ice-chains began to melt, dripping away rapidly.

'Don't be sad, Kari,' she said. 'It's all over.'

Surprised, he managed to smile back. 'Yes. It's over. Tell Wulfgar what you've seen. Tell him we're coming home.'

Fading before their eyes she reached out to touch him. 'All of you? Are you all coming?'

'All of us.'

And then the chair was empty, and Jessa imagined with sudden clarity the girl lying in that bed in the hold; how she would be waking now, sitting up, stiff and hungry; how she would race downstairs, into the silence and cold of the hall, to Wulfgar . . .

'What about the others?' she asked aloud.

'Gudrun's spell faded with her,' Kari said. He sat down against the wall, knees up. 'They'll all be awaking now – the noise and the warmth will come flooding back. All their souls will return to them; the hold will be as we always knew it – busy, warm, alive.'

'In fact by the time we get back,' Skapti said slyly, 'they'll have forgotten all about it.'

'And us,' Jessa muttered. 'It's a long way.'

'Indeed it is. And there are places we'll go a long way round,' Brochael rumbled.

They all laughed, and fell silent.

After a moment Kari got up and went out into the hall. Brochael gazed after him, uneasily.

'Let him go,' Skapti muttered.

'He's too quiet. I thought he'd be . . . happy.'

Skapti rubbed his unshaven chin. 'Give him time, Brochael. All his life she's been there, a threat, a torment. When a weight comes off your back you're often too stiff to stand up at once.'

It was Jessa who went after him, much later. She found him standing at the side of the bier, looking down, quite still. Beside him, Jessa was silent a moment. Then she said, 'Where is she, Kari?'

He twisted the frayed end of his sleeve around his fingers. 'I don't know, Jessa,' he said, finally. 'I stole her soul and locked it into a crystal, locked it deep, with tight spells. But he's taken it back into that world, it's lost there, and I don't know how to find it again.' He looked up, intently. 'Perhaps Moongarm was wise. Now she's neither dead nor alive. Because I couldn't have killed her, Jessa.'

They turned and walked back into the little room. Brochael looked up at them.

'We leave tomorrow, after we've all slept. Unless you want your kingdom.'

Kari laughed, suddenly, 'Grettir can have it. Thrasirshall is my kingdom. And you're its only subject.'

They all laughed then, Brochael hearty with relief, and the sound echoed in the empty rooms and halls of the palace, and Jessa thought that it was a strange, new sound here, and wherever they were the white people heard it with surprise. She caught Hakon's eye.

'You never got round to naming your sword.'

213

'Ah, but I have.'

'Tell us then.'

Awkwardly, he touched the hilt. 'You'll laugh.'

'No we won't.'

'Well, at first I thought of Bear-bane . . .'

Despite herself, Jessa giggled.

'Not bad,' Skapti conceded.

'. . . And then Snake-stabber. But I didn't think that was any good . . .'

'It's not.'

'. . . so I thought of Dream-breaker.'

'Why that?' she asked.

'Because in my dream I fell from the bridge, but the sword saved me.' He smiled at them, shyly. 'What do you think?'

'It's a fine name,' Skapti said.

Kari nodded, and Brochael laughed. 'I never thought we'd make it, then.'

'Oh I did,' Jessa said, putting her arms round them both. 'I always did.'